THE UN.

CHASING CATS

FROM USA TODAY BESTSELLING AUTHOR
ERIN BEDFORD

Chasing Cats © 2019 Embrace the Fantasy Publishing, LLC

Also by Erin Bedford

The Underground Series
Chasing Rabbits
Chasing Cats
Chasing Princes
Chasing Shadows
Chasing Hearts
The Crimes of Alice

The Mary Wiles Chronicles
Marked by Hell
Bound by Hell
Deceived by Hell
Tempted by Hell

Starcrossed Dragons
Riding Lightning
Grinding Frost
Swallowing Fire
Pounding Earth

The Celestial War Chronicles
Song of Blood and Fire

The Crimson Fold
Until Midnight
Until Dawn
Until Sunset
Until Twilight

Curse of the Fairy Tales
Rapunzel Untamed
Rapunzel Unveiled

Her Angels
Heaven's Embrace
Heaven's A Beach
Heaven's Most Wanted

House of Durand
Indebted to the Vampires
Wanted by the Vampires

Academy of Witches
Witching On A Star
As You Witch
Witch You Were Here

Granting Her Wish
Vampire CEO

THE UNDERGROUND BOOK TWO

CHASING CATS

FROM USA TODAY BESTSELLING AUTHOR
ERIN BEDFORD

CHAPTER

HOME AGAIN

HE WAS STARING again. Lately, every time I looked up Mr. Blue Eyes was sitting in the tree outside my kitchen window.

As my constant shadow in the Underground, I was shocked to say the least, to find out my feathered friend was indeed my fiancé. I knew the UnSeelie Prince had the ability to change form, but it kind of left me peeved to know that he had been following me around the Underground.

The bright blue eyes had darkened to Dorian's usual midnight blue and were set in a feathered head that cocked to the side when it saw me looking. I frowned; even in owl form Dorian still exuded arrogance and overall disdain for the human world. His presence was becoming a regular unwelcome occurrence for me.

I wasn't surprised. Had I really thought I could slip out of the Underground without anyone noticing? I knew there would be repercussions, but at the time all I could think about was getting home to my world— well, the human world. Chess' outstretched hand had been a Godsend and the easiest alternative to the pressure that had been weighing on me.

I hadn't been home from the Underground for more than a day when my feathered keeper showed up. He never tried approached me, not like I thought he would.

Back in the Underground, he'd been so determined to make me see how sorry he was, how much he wanted to start things up again. Even though his constant watching was on the creepy side, it was a relief that was all he was doing.

Luckily, my Fae mother, Tatiana, Queen of the Seelie Court and the main Fae I was avoiding, hadn't reactivated the curse on Dorian in light of my disappearing act. I was sure his mother had some say in the matter as well.

Mab, the UnSeelie Queen, like her son, tended to have a temper. I doubted she would let her precious baby boy be blamed for my human flakiness. They probably thought Dorian was their best chance at getting me to come home.

Not that he has tried.

"Back again, I see. He doesn't seem to get the hint, does he?" I jumped in place at the sound of Chess' voice purring right beside my ear.

"Don't do that!" I spun around and smacked him with a dishtowel as he chuckled. My angry face threatened to fall when I took in the sight of him.

Half Seelie, half UnSeelie, Chess was nothing like the Cheshire cat from the classic fairy tale. His pale pink hair was loose around his broad shoulders. His muscular chest was covered with a cream-colored, cotton sleeveless shirt that left his biceps bare and flexing. The faint scars that crisscrossed over his upper body barely peeked out from the slight split in the neck of the collar. A corded braid was wrapped around his neck and hung loosely down his chest. It brushed the top of his fitted rose-colored pants, where his stripped tail was wrapped around his waist. His usual knee-high boots were swapped out for a pair of brown ankle boots.

I fought the smile that threatened to creep up my face when his purple and pink striped ears twitched on his head while he smirked down at me.

"I'm serious. What if someone had been here? They could have seen you. Then how would I explain that? Oh hi, mom, this is my friend Chess. He's a cat Fae from another world. What's a Fae you ask? Well, they are magical creatures that could kill you in an instant, but don't worry, the only thing in danger is your underpants. Yeah, that will go over well." I rolled my eyes.

"Oh, don't worry so much, pet. You'll get wrinkles." He rubbed his clawed finger between my scrunched up brows.

I didn't want to be distracted, so I shrugged his hand away and turned back to the sink and the dishes in it. You'd think that as the Seelie Princess I wouldn't have to do my own chores, but since I was in deep denial of that responsibility, lowly domestic tasks like dishes had to be done.

"Don't tell me you aren't happy to see me?" Chess pouted in a too cute tone that made my insides melt.

Cheshire S. Cat knew just how attractive he was and didn't need to know how his very presence caused a fire to ignite in me. I was in an ongoing battle with my libido since meeting the Fae, but I hadn't lost yet,

10

even if the Fae could tell how I was feeling by my smell alone.

As if reading my mind, Chess pressed his nose to my hair and inhaled, growling slightly. Damn those Fae senses.

"You're so responsive. I've barely touched you, and you already smell so tantalizing."

I shivered against his breath on my neck.

"I can't wait to find out how you'll react to all my ministrations." His chuckle was dark and invited naughty thoughts to play in my mind. His tail unwrapped from his waist and slid across the skin between my green polo shirt and jeans.

His hands replaced his tail, pulling my back flush against his front. I slammed the pot I had been cleaning down into the sink harder than I meant. I tried to focus on the sink full of dishes and not the tingling of my skin or the pooling of my nether regions.

"Don't you have somewhere to be?" I was proud that I was able to speak without my voice shaking, let alone being able to sound snappy. "An Underground to moderate. Payments to defile?"

I winced when the last part came out bitter. Jealous? Who, me?

Chess' hands stilled on my waist, and he stepped back from me to hop up on the

11

counter next to the sink. He leaned back on one hand until he was able to meet my eyes. I kept my gaze down so he couldn't see the emotions flipping through them. He brushed a piece of my pale blonde hair behind my ear, the color a daily reminder that my time in the Underground wasn't a dream. Not that the memories of my life as a Fae Princess would let that be a possibility.

When I had been sucked into that rabbit hole, I hadn't expected to come out alive, let alone with a new hairdo and a whole new set of baggage. Lucky for me, it wasn't unusual for someone to change their hair color so drastically. Also, the fact that my human mother had a cow when she found out I had colored my red hair blonde was the only good thing to have come of it. If only my Fae life was so easily managed.

"Jealousy becomes you, your highness. I especially love it when you show your claws," he said. I snorted, not falling victim to his game. He continued after a moment, "Besides, there's nothing to moderate. The queens are on speaking terms again, and all is right in the Underground. There's no need for dear old Chess anymore."

I frowned at the resentment in his voice. It wasn't the first time the feline had hinted at his dissatisfaction toward the Fae Courts and their rulers. It made me wonder what happened between them to make him hold such disdain.

My eyes strayed to his scars, and I asked the one question I'd been dying to ask since we met, "How did these happen?"

I reached out a finger to trace along one peeking out from his shirt.

He caught my hand in his and brought it up to his mouth to nip at my fingers. "It happened a very long time ago, before I had the position of moderator to protect me."

"Protect you? From what?" His mouth on my hand was distracting me enough to make my voice come out low and breathy, but not enough for me to give up my curiosity.

"If you are so concerned for my wellbeing, I could give you a thorough look at my person to satisfy your curiosity." He pulled my top half forward with a tug of my hand until we were inches from each other. "That is, as long as I get equal payment in return."

"Payment?" I muttered, my eyes entirely too focused on his tempting lips rather than his words, or that he was deflecting my questions again.

His mouth coasted over mine, a ghost of a whisper, his words hot against my lips.

"Yes, a complete examination will be required in return." He slid down from the counter to press his length against me. My breath hitched when my hands landed on his chest, the feel of him hard beneath my palms. "But I must warn you, I will be vigorous in my search."

I gulped at his words as his clawed hand tilted my face up. I knew he was going to kiss me, and part of me tried to remember why it was a bad idea when his lips descended onto mine. Before I could sink into the kiss, something slammed behind me. I jumped and pulled back. Chess smirked, and I followed his gaze to where Dorian stood in his entire UnSeelie splendor.

His inky black hair fell over his equally dark silk shirt. Had he always dressed like a Goth? How did I not notice that before? His pants were only a slight shade dimmer than his shirt; if you could get darker than blackest black, and were tucked into shiny, leather knee-high boots. The Fae may have some modern amenities, but some of their clothing still screamed otherworldly. My fiancé was no exception.

"Get away from her, half-breed." The sound of his voice was sharp but held forbidden promises.

I felt Chess tense beside me before his usual fang tipped grin slid over his face. "Your highness, what brings you here? Aren't you supposed to be guarding something?"

My breath held for the reaction I knew would come at Chess' goading. Short tempered and impatient had always been Dorian's worst traits. In some ways, the curse had been good for him.

Dorian needed to learn to regulate his temper, as I had often told him. I would have thought that having such a restriction on his emotions would cause some of his control to be better, but it didn't seem like it—if the tightening of his jaw was any indication.

He had been blamed for my Fae body's suicide in the most torturous of fashions. Forced into exile from the UnSeelie Court, he was tasked to watch the outskirts to keep out the human riff-raff. To my mother, being exiled wasn't enough. She'd branded his beautiful aristocratic face with a curse, forcing him to be happy about his punishment, though most of the time it had come out more creepy than happy. He

15

hadn't been able to mourn my death or have any other emotional releases. It really was no wonder he was so uptight.

He glared at Chess and then stormed across the room in a cloud of fury. I stepped forward, placing myself between the two before they could start anything.

Dorian glanced down at me before snarling at Chess, "You would do well to remember your place, half-breed."

"Chess," I retorted. Dorian's burning gaze landed on me, but I didn't shy away. "His name isn't half-breed—it's Chess. And it was a perfectly logical question. What are you doing here?"

Dorian opened his mouth to respond and then snapped it closed, his lips twisting into a frown. "You know very well why I am here."

"Actually, no. I don't." Crossing my hands over my chest, I leveled my eyes at him and tapped my foot. I could practically feel Chess crowing in glee behind me and was half tempted to let them have at it. It would at least be entertaining for me, and if they were shirtless, hot as hell.

His dark eyes looked over my head as he growled, "You are not safe on your own here. I am here for your protect—"

I snorted, cutting him off. "More like to spy for the courts."

Growing tired of the conversation, I moved away from both Fae to finish the dishes, which at this rate, weren't going to be done until Christmas. Why did the dishwasher have to break today?

"I am not spying for the courts," Dorian continued as if I hadn't dismissed him altogether. "We are simply not confident in the human realms ability to keep you safe."

"And that has nothing to do with them wanting you to convince Kat to come home?" Chess asked. "Tell me, your highness, are you here for your court or hers? Who holds your leash now that you are no longer bound to the outskirts?"

The dish in my hand paused, suspended mid-air, as I waited for his answer. I didn't know why I cared so much. I didn't love him. I couldn't. Not like he wanted me to, anyway.

"No one holds my leash, Cheshire." The way he said the name was filled with so much venom, I could feel the sting of it on my skin. "I am here for Lynne's safety and no other reason."

"Kat," I bit out.

"What?" Dorian barked at me.

I could feel my magic building inside me, morphing my anger into rage. He still didn't get it. My hands gripped the counter until my knuckles turned white. I just wanted him to understand. I wasn't her. I mean, I was, but I wasn't. It was all very complicated, and I always gave myself a headache when thinking too hard on it.

"What did you say, Lynne?"

The moment he said that name again, the magic in me broke loose. Every dish in the house flew from their places in the cabinets. They crashed to the ground in a symphony of glass. Pots and pans clanged and dented as they were thrown across the room.

"Kat?" Chess' voice filled my ears, and I unclenched my hands from the counter. A heaviness I hadn't known I felt was suddenly lighter than before.

Turning from the counter, I surveyed the destruction I had caused in my little outburst. The entire kitchen was trashed. Not only had all the dishes been damaged, but also everything from the refrigerator had been spilled onto the floor. Leftover spaghetti lay in a goopy red mess on the tiles mixed with the jar of pickles I always kept handy. Now, what was I going to eat at four in the morning?

The two Fae stood in the middle of the room, concern filling their faces.

I gave an aggravated sigh and waved them off with a, "I'm fine," before I bent to start picking up my mess.

"You're wound too tightly, my kitty Kat." Chess chuckled, even as Dorian sent him a scathing glare. "You have magic now. You can't neglect it, or it will find a way to get loose."

"Well, as much as I despise saying it, the cat is right," Dorian said with a huff. "Though, I do not understand how this has happened." That made two of us. "The fact of the matter is, your magic is returning to you, and I have little doubt it will stop there."

"What do you mean?" I paused on the floor where I was making a pile of dishes.

"Though you reside in a human body, I believe your other Fae abilities may materialize, and you must be prepared for it."

I glanced over at Chess who was helping put some of the broken glass into a pile. He gave me a solemn nod to confirm Dorian's words. I didn't know why I trusted Chess' word over Dorian's; he hadn't been any more honest with me. In fact, I didn't know anything about him, and he didn't exist in the memories I had from when I was the Seelie Princess.

"Why don't I remember Chess from before?" I didn't want to have the headache causing talk about my new powers and what they could mean to my human life.

Dorian crossed his arms over his broad chest, his eyes alighting with mirth. "I would not imagine you would. He was not born during your time, Lynne."

My right eye twitched at the name again, but I chose to ignore it in lieu of getting answers. "But why –" To my irritation, Dorian cut me off.

"Which brings me to the other reason I am here." He turned back to the cat in question. "You have been summoned to the Seelie Court. Since no one has been able to locate you, and I had no doubt that you would show back up here eventually, I volunteered as messenger."

"What can I say? I'm a sucker for a beautiful woman." Chess gave me a fanged grin, the heat in his eyes more for Dorian's benefit than my own.

Anger pulsated off Dorian in waves, making his hair move as if there was a breeze, but I knew from my own experience with magic, there wasn't.

"You will keep your hands off Lynne. She does not belong to you." His words sliced the air like a knife in my lungs.

Chess smirked. "She doesn't belong to you either, your highness. What I do, or do not do, is all up to her." He winked at me, and I flushed. God, he was a flirt. But Dorian didn't see the humor in his words.

"Lynne is mine!" His voice vibrated through the room, and the picture frames fell from their places on the wall.

I was done. So done. Monumentally done.

I grabbed the closest pan to me and stood to my feet, waving it like a weapon in the air. "Stop calling me that! I am not yours. I am far from yours. I'm Kat. Kat. Got that?"

His eyes widened as I jabbed the pan at him. A wince filled his face at every jab. Was he always such a wimp? It's not like it was a knife or something it was just a pan...an iron pan that was turning molten hot in my grip!

"Motherfucker." I dropped the pan, howling, my injured hand held out in front of me.

Every inch of the skin that had been in contact with the pan turned a nasty shade of red. Angry blisters appeared on my palm, threatening to pop at any moment.

"I knew this would happen." Dorian sighed and tried to reach out to grab my wrist, but Chess beat him to it.

"I'll handle this." Chess gave me a small, reassuring smile before he narrowed his gaze at Dorian. "Don't you have somewhere to be, your highness?"

Every time Chess said the honorific, it always had a slight condescending quality to it. I was surprised Dorian let him get away with it. He was never one to let someone act above their station, especially a half-breed.

Crossing his arms over his chest, his silken shirt pulled tight across his muscles, Dorian returned Chess' look with an equally haughty one. "Not as of this moment, but you do, half—" He cut off at my warning frown. "Cheshire and you better not keep your Queen waiting."

Chess' jaw tightened as did his grip on me. "She is not my queen, any more than she is yours."

"Be that as it may, at one time, she was all of our queen, and unless you would like a reminder, I would suggest you make haste. I can take care of Katherine," he said, giving me a pointed look, like I should praise him for remembering to use the correct name, "as I always have."

Chess made a sound of disagreement before turning to me. "I won't be gone long, and if you need anything..." His green eyes locked onto Dorian. "If you need anything at all, just call."

I pushed him away with my good hand. "Go. Go. Don't keep my mother waiting. I'll be fine."

Chess gave me one last cursory glance before turning on his heel and disappearing into thin air. I stared down at my injured appendage with a wince. My hand hurt, my kitchen was a mess, and I was utterly alone with the last person in this, or any realm, I wanted to talk to. Great.

"COME." DORIAN GESTURED for me to have a seat at the table.

I eyed the chair, shuffling from one foot to the other. While my hand hurt like hell, I really had no inclination to sit down and hash out our issues, which I was sure he would try to do.

"You know…" I cleared my throat. "I'm fine, really. I just need to get the first aid kit out of the bathroom, and I'll be right as rain. There's no need for you to hang around."

His eyes narrowed at my obvious attempt to get rid of him. "Nonsense. I am here. There is no reason you should endure on your own."

"Really, Dorian. I'm fine. I just need—"

"Katherine. While I understand your need for independence, your measly human medicine will not suffice to heal such a Fae-related injury, and unless you want it to spread, which it will no doubt do if not treated properly, I suggest you—how do you say—suck it up."

If the thought of the blisters spreading wasn't enough of a determining factor, the sharp tone in his voice told me I was wasting my time trying to argue with him.

I threw my good hand up in the air with an exasperated sigh. "Fine."

"Good. Now, sit." With a twist of his wrist, a container with some kind of beige crème in it appeared.

I dropped into the chair at the kitchen table with a huff. So much for avoiding the awkward conversation he would no doubt try to start. What was I going to say? What was he going to say? You'd think having my memories back would make things easier, but it didn't. Not really. I had a hard time explaining it to myself, let alone to someone else. Especially someone who wanted the girl I used to be to be real.

"I cannot treat your hand if you do not give it to me." The laughter in Dorian's voice was not lost on me. At least one of us thought this situation was funny.

I hesitated before gingerly holding my hand out to him across the table. It was odd to see the Dark Prince, dressed in his regal attire, sitting in one of the mismatched kitchen chairs as if it were a throne under his delightful tush. It was hard to believe he was really here in the human world.

"Why do you look at me in such a manner?" He twisted the top of the container; a sharp flowery smell assaulted my senses. Angelica? It was well known in the Fae world to counteract iron poisoning. I had always hated that smell. Wait. Did I?

I shook my head to clear the befuddlement that was my past life and met his bemused sapphire eyes.

"Like what?"

"As if you are plotting my demise." Dipping his long slender fingers into the container, he then began to spread it across the festering blisters on my palm. The crème felt cool against my burning skin, and I fought against the urge to moan out loud.

"I don't know what you are talking about," I muttered, blushing even though I hadn't been thinking anything close to that.

He gave an exasperated sigh, pausing his ministrations.

"I used to be able to read your expressions so well. Now..." he trailed off, the forlorn expression not making his face any less handsome.

"It's different."

"Yes. Different." His voice was soft as his hand resumed stroking mine. This time, it was more for the sake of touching than healing.

I eased my hand out of his, the tension in the room became stifling.

"Thanks," I mumbled as I stood from the table, needing to get some distance between us.

"Lynne. I mean, Katherine." He had that look in his eyes that said my luck was out, and he wanted to talk.

"Don't. Just don't." I put my good hand up to stop him as he stood from his seat. His height towered over me, making the room feel smaller.

"We need to talk about this. You cannot go on pretending like I do not exist." He grabbed my uninjured hand, pulling it to his chest. "Like we never existed."

His heart beat beneath my palm, and it caused an ache in my own. I'd have laughed if the moment hadn't been such a serious one. Pretend like he didn't exist? That wasn't likely, especially with how he had taken it upon himself to be my shadow. I could no more pretend he wasn't real than I could stop the memories from stalking me in my dreams.

Since I had come back, there was not a moment when I closed my eyes where my dreams were my own. It had become so bad that I was afraid to fall asleep at night, because I knew what I would see. It was like a hundred years of being suppressed made that part of me need reconfirmation that we were alive. So I was treated to a reel of my life as Lynne over and over again. The good, the bad, and the heart wrenching painful moments that had me jerking awake in the middle of the night. Seeing him like this was almost more than I could bear.

I extracted my hand from him with my heart in my throat.

"I can't." My voice was a helpless whimper that I hated.

"Cannot what?" The pleading in his voice made the whole situation even worse.

"Do this. Us." I turned from him, wrapping my arms around myself, being cautious of my still tender hand.

"But why? Why can you not give us a chance? I know you are not the same woman, but—"

I spun around. "Do you? Because from what I've seen; you don't seem to get it at all. I'm not. I can't be the princess you fell in love with. I'm not her."

"But she is in there somewhere. You have her memories. Her feelings." He placed his hands on my upper arms and pulled me close. "Who is to say you cannot feel the same thing for me?"

I let him hold me close to him. The beat of his heart pounded in my ears. It would be so easy to pretend. To just pick up where Lynne had left off, but it wasn't that simple. Not only was I human, but also I wasn't even sure who I was anymore. What part of me was real? What feelings were mine and which ones were hers?

I swallowed hard and pushed away from him, tears pricking my eyes. "I can't."

"Try, please. For me," he begged. It seemed so wrong to hear those words from him. He was the UnSeelie Prince; he shouldn't be begging anyone, least of all me.

"I think you should go. Don't you have a kingdom to rule?" I quirked my brow, trying to soften the blow. "Your mother must be beside herself with worry. Why aren't you with her?"

Dorian's jaw tightened. "I have not been to see her yet."

"What? Why?" My mouth popped open in surprise.

From the way Mab had acted in the garden, I would have thought she would be the first person he would see once his curse was lifted.

"I did not think she would want to see me."

I almost laughed until I saw his face. "You're serious? Why would you think that? Of course she wants to see you!"

Dorian and his mother had the kind of relationship I had always envied. The dark and domineering exterior was just a show for their soft and warm insides. I had never seen any mother love her child as much as Mab did Dorian—unlike my mother, human or Fae, whose exterior was as cold on the inside as out.

This time, he turned from me, hiding his face from my view. "You would not understand. You were not here when they found out what happened. It is—"

"Complicated. Yeah, I know. God, do I know." I blew out a shaky laugh.

Complicated seemed to define my life right now, and it seemed like I wasn't the only one.

"I should take my leave."

He moved toward the door, and before I could stop myself, I called out after him.

"Wait."

He stopped in his tracks, and I instantly regretted speaking.

"Was this not what you wanted?" The muscles in his back tensed.

I opened my mouth but had no words. I didn't know why I told him to wait. I had asked him to leave, but knowing he had suffered because of me made the emotions I thought were buried under a thick blanket of stubbornness billow up.

"Are you coming back?"

Coward.

His shoulders bunched up as if surprised by my words. "Do you wish me to?"

Well, that was the million-dollar question. The fact that I couldn't answer that one question said how screwed up in the head I was. While the Fae part of me still remembered the gut-wrenching feel of his betrayal, the human part of me was solely focused on the memory of Dorian himself. I knew what it felt like to kiss him, to touch him, to be touched by him. It didn't help that the latest dream had focused on the brooding Fae Prince with a lot fewer clothes and a lot sweatier goodness. The memory of it was enough to make my insides quiver.

A growl ripped from his throat, and before I even recognized the feeling, his hands were buried in my hair, and my face was yanked up to his.

The first time he had kissed me in my human form was in a memory. My own memory, to be exact. I had fallen through a looking glass in the Seelie Court that was used to view whatever the looker wanted. I had unfortunately been thinking of the UnSeelie Prince, and though I hadn't known it at the time, I ended up in one of my own memories.

But unlike then, where his kiss had been long and lingering; this one was demanding, and almost punishing, yet it held an underlying uncertainty. It was that uncertainty that caused my hand to curl into the front of his shirt and kiss him back. I sank into the kiss even though I knew it was hypocritical. I'd pushed him away over and over with claims of not feeling anything for him, but it was a lie. I felt more for him than I was comfortable with, and that was reason enough to keep him at arm's length.

Nothing good would come from this. I was human. He was a Fae prince. One that didn't really see me: Kat, the human. He only saw Lynne, and it was that part that just wanted to give in to him.

Because it was easy. It was familiar. Even if it was wrong.

With that thought, I pushed him away from me, panting, as I looked anywhere but at him. "Please go."

He stood there, no doubt dumbfounded at my sudden change. "But we—"

"It was a mistake," I cut in. I licked my swollen lips and tried to keep my voice steady. "It won't happen again."

This time, when he grabbed me by the arms, it wasn't gentle. His pinching grip jerked my eyes to his in a smoldering glare.

"I could make you, you know." His eyes glittered with anger. "I could make you love me. You are human now. So weak. So easily manipulated."

His magic pheromones pulsed me. My breath caught and parts of me that had been cooling off flared to life.

The press of his power might have caused a physical reaction, but the anger that flared to life brought my own magic with it. I let it rise to the surface, causing my skin to crackle. His hands loosened before tightening once more, unrelenting against my warning.

33

"You would not even know the difference," he bit out through clenched teeth as his magic pushed down on me further, making the room feel like it was losing oxygen by the second.

I surprised myself, because instead of lashing out with my magic, I let it melt away.

Meeting his eyes with a level stare, I said, "Then do it. If that is all that matters to you, do it. I'll be a mindless puppet, completely at your disposal."

His expression softened slightly, his grip a little less pinching. I knew he wouldn't do it. He couldn't do it. It wouldn't be real. Not really. I'd been on both ends of Fae pheromones and knew what they could do to a human. Prolonged exposure could ruin them, both mind and body. They wasted away, pining after the Fae that had exposed them. It was one of the reasons why the Fae were forbidden to use their pheromones for anything but dire situations. At least, that was the way it was a hundred years ago.

A throat cleared behind him, interrupting our stare down. "Uh, ye highness?"

Not taking his eyes from me, Dorian answered the voice I couldn't have been happier to hear, "What is it, troll?"

I frowned at Dorian's degrading tone. Mop was not a troll. He was a brownie. A short, little cocoa-colored Fae with a dark beard and even darker eyes. His red overalls matched his red hat, and his feet were bare. He had been my constant companion through my recent adventure in the Underground and always seemed to get there in the nick of time. This was one of those times.

"Hello, Mop." I smiled, stepping around a perturbed Dorian.

"Lady." He nodded at me, his gaze still on his prince. "Ye highness, I don't be meanin' to intrude, but ye mother be askin' for ye and sent me to relieve ye."

"Relieve him?" I cast an irritated glance back at Dorian. "Why would you need to relieve him?"

"Uh..." Mop looked to Dorian for an answer, seeming to not want to give away more than the prince had let on.

"So, your highness." I crossed my arms over my chest and waited. I used his title for the sake of the others in the room. Names have power, and you didn't want to give the wrong person that kind of power over you. Not that I didn't trust Mop to keep his mouth shut. It was better safe than sorry.

You never knew who could be listening, though.

"It's for your own good." His voice was short and left no room for argument, but I was never one to let that stop me.

"So you've what? Been babysitting me? I'm an adult. I don't need a keeper." I flipped my hair over my shoulder with more flair than required.

"As I can see." He looked me up and down in a salacious enough way that even Chess would have blushed. Mop gave an uncomfortable cough. "But the fact of the matter is, you're the Seelie Princess. The only heir to the Seelie Court and now that you are back, you have to understand that your mother—everyone—is reluctant to let you go again. Especially with Alice on the loose and the shadows gathering forces."

That had my attention. I had only been gone a few days and already things in the Underground were falling apart. Fuck me.

CHAPTER

FALLING APART

THE SHADOWS. IN my time as the Seelie Princess, I had only heard whispers of them. The Fae so monstrous, so corrupted that even the Seelie Queen didn't trust them to be thrown into her mirror prison.

I'd been told the Shadows were exactly that. Shadows of their former selves made from the black abyss they had been exiled to so long ago.

Sheltered as I was before, I had never stepped outside the palace walls, except for the times I snuck out to meet Dorian in the Orchard. It was easy to pretend there wasn't pain and suffering in my kingdom when I didn't have to see it. But as a human that all changed.

The Shadows were no strangers to me. I knew their plea. Their wants and desires. Me being one of those primary ones.

I could still feel their burning touch on my skin. Their promise to give me everything I ever wanted. To make me their queen. I had promised I'd think about it, but when you are facing down pure evil, you will swear just about anything to get away.

"What's happened?" I targeted my question toward Mop and hoped it came across curious and not at all nervous.

Mop glanced at Dorian as if asking for permission.

"Yes, tell her, troll. Tell her how her actions have consequences." His dark eyes narrowed at me. "Rules are rules for a reason. Even for you."

"Pfft. Rules are meant to be broken." I cocked my hip to the side, trying to seem confident and not at all guilty.

"I do not remember you being so cocky before. It must be the human in you." Dorian sneered before he whipped his arm around, transforming into the beautiful barn owl.

"Hey, you better not poop on my floor!" I hollered after him as he swooped through the kitchen and out the open back door.

Marching over to the door, I slammed it shut and locked it for good measure. "Good riddance."

"Ye really shouldn't treat his highness so poorly. Ye don't know what he went through after ye left."

Guilt gnawed at me from Mop's chastising. The thought of causing Dorian pain still made my insides ache and the thought that he was punished because of my irrational thinking made it even worse. I felt bad for the guy, but he still irritated the shit out me.

"He started it," I pouted with a childish tone.

"Ye don't need to be lettin' him rile ye up. Nothin' more than children, ye are." Mop muttered the last bit to himself before plopping down in a kitchen chair.

"Hey now, I wouldn't say that! And shouldn't you be treating me with reverence and fear? I am royalty, you know." I lifted my chin and gave my best regal expression.

"Bah!" He snorted. "Bein' royalty ain't got nothin' to do with who ye are."

"And who exactly am I?"

"Lady, 'course." He shook his head, the red cap swishing back and forth. "Just cause ye be havin' the soul of the Seelie Princess, don't mean ye're her."

Finally! Someone got it. I could kiss Mop with how happy his words made me, but I wouldn't because that would be weird, and I was limited to how many people were on my side right now.

"Besides," he continued. "I doubt ye have much power considerin' ye be human and all."

"Not true! See all this." I gestured to the mess in the kitchen. "All me, buddy."

"My point exactly. Ye might be havin' the abilities of the princess but ye ain't knowin' how to use 'em. " He cringed as he seemed to take in the disaster that was my kitchen for the first time. "Or how to be controlin' em. Ye no better off than one of thems younglins."

"Well, then, why don't you teach me?" I was getting tired of being called a child. I was a grown ass woman. Take my breasts for instance. You didn't see fabulous knockers like these on a ten-year-old!

"I've told ye before. I be a lower Fae. I wouldn't be knowin' the first thing 'bout ye powers."

"So what? Don't you have any powers? I don't remember there being that much of a difference between the lower Fae and the higher Fae. Not that my mother dared to let her precious baby girl be exposed to them."

40

I let the bitterness toward the Seelie Queen fill my voice.

It was a wonder I ever made friends at all with how locked down I had been. Not only was I restricted to the palace, but I was only allowed in certain areas. More often than not you would have found me in the gardens. The library and the dining room were the only other rooms I was allowed in, besides my own quarters. I was surprised any of the Fae knew me at all since the Court room was strictly forbidden.

Once I had asked why I wasn't allowed in Court and my mother had returned my question with a condescending laugh. "The Underground is a cruel world, darling. You have to know how to play the game to survive."

She'd gazed down at me as if there was something in me lacking, and for all I knew, there probably was. Not that I would want whatever she deemed worthy of going to Court. Bunch of self-absorbed vultures.

"Now hold ye horses." Mop's irritated growl pulled me from my thoughts. "I didn't say I not be havin' any powers. Just not the kind ye be havin'." He held his hands up in defense.

"Then what are they? And what about Trip? What are his powers?" Trip was the

41

white opalaught that started this whole mess when I had mistaken him for a rabbit. As far as I could tell, his only ability was being able to chew through any garden wire that I threw at him.

"Ye humans, always with the questions. Unfortunately, bein' part Fae hasn't changed that rude habit." Mop glared at me. "Since ye apparently don't remember, askin' someone's powers be like askin' their true name. It be rude, and fights have started over less."

I had the decency to look ashamed. I did remember the rules, but the human half of me didn't have a filter or care as much about them. Though, my diarrhea of a mouth didn't always listen to me.

"Well, if you won't answer that, how about where is Trip?" I searched the room for my white-eared friend as if he was hiding somewhere nearby. "Isn't he usually with you?"

"I be imagin' he be with Hare." His voice sounded less offended now and more distracted. "Hatter be actin' strange the last few days."

I'd never actually talked to Hatter. I'd only seen him once at the Mourning party. The party the Seelie Fae threw in honor of—well, me. As parties went, I wasn't impressed anymore now than I had been then. From what I had seen of Hatter, he hadn't seemed to like being there either. I wouldn't know one way or another if he were acting strangely or not.

"What is considered strange for Hatter? He looked kind of pissed off last time we saw him." The serious expression on the tall silver-haired Hatter flashed through my mind.

Mop barked out a laugh. "I'd imagine he would be surrounded by all thems Seelie. He might look like them, but he ain't got the patience for their high and mighty outlooks toward the rest of the Fae residence."

"But he's high Fae, too, isn't he?" From what I knew, most high Fae seemed more humanoid and less like animals, unlike the lower Fae. Not that I'd met many. In fact, I was beginning to think I didn't know a whole lot about my own world.

"Hatter be High Fae, just like ye are, but unlike them, he prefers the company of the Lower Fae. If ye could call that party of lunatics Fae." He snorted.

Having witnessed their crazed antics, I couldn't exactly argue.

"So, how is he different now?" I tried to change the subject back.

Mop took his hat off his head and wrung it between his hands. For the first time since Dorian left, Mop looked worried.

"Could be many things," he muttered to himself as if forgetting I was even there.

"Like?" I pressed, taking a step closer to him.

"Well." He turned his hat around in his hands, staring down at it with such intensity it was making me worry. "There be all thems disappearances as of late, and then there be the rumors."

"Disappearances? Rumors? What do you mean? What's happened?" I had a sinking feeling that I knew what he was going to say.

"First, there be Twinkle," he murmured with his eyes downcast. "Then Door Mouse up and disappeared. No note, no nothin' and ye know it had to be thems Shadows, but no one be certain since no one be seein' nothin'. It can only mean..."

"What? What does it mean?" I urged him to continue.

He leaned in close to me, lowering his voice so I had to strain to hear him. "Thems Shadows be taken corporeal form."

I swallowed hard, trying to act surprised. "And that's bad?"

Mop jumped up from his seat, waving his arms around in the air. "'Course that be bad! Separately, they be just an annoyance. Only a threat to those who don't be knowin' the rules. But together?" He visibly shuddered. "Ye don't want to be knowin' the havoc they could ensue."

Oh, I was sure I could imagine it since I was there when it happened. I remembered what it was like to be at the mercy of the horde of lost Fae. The thought of their touch on my skin still gave me the urge to take a scalding hot shower. I knew for a fact that they had a body now, one attractive, Fae male body to be exact. He made my skin crawl even more so than the formless blob did.

"And ye know Alice had to be responsible for it." The brownie spat her name out like a plague to the Fae world. Which, in a way, she was.

The Alice I had read about in human fairy tales wasn't as innocent as Lewis Carroll would have us believe. One thing he did get right was she was a tiresome little snot. She was as manipulative as any Fae, and since that was exactly what she had wished to be when she got involved with Dorian and my affairs, I guessed it was only fitting.

"Why do you think Alice had anything to do with it?" She kind of had a part in it, but since I wasn't about to tell him I was the one who helped the Shadows take their solid form, it was best to play along.

He gave me a look of exasperation as if I should have been able to guess what was inside his head. "Don't ye find it being a bit funny that when ye let her loose, the Shadows be gaining their form?"

"But I don't see how that matters? I thought no one even knew why Alice was in the Hall of Mirrors?" I tried to redirect the topic from the Shadows. I didn't know how much longer I could evade Mop's questions without outright lying. I didn't know how well his sense of smell was but if it was anything like Chess' the changes in my scent from my lie wouldn't be hidden for long.

"That be before ye be turnin' all royalty and such. Now that ye be alive, and Alice be free, anybody who knew anything be flappin' their jaws on what they know." He crossed his arms over his chest as if he were completely disgusted with the whole affair.

Faes don't make mistakes, my ass. Dorian and my mother thought they had erased all traces of what happened to Alice

46

and me after I, well, went away. I didn't really like to think about the fact that I had actually tried to off myself. Or the other me did. The human me was riding the denial train with no visible stops in sight.

"The problem be," Mop continued. "How did she do it?"

"Do what?"

"Be makin' them come together as one. It would be takin' a lot of magic to make them into one form, let alone gettin' them to agree to bein' one form. I didn't think that child be havin' what it takes to get them agreein' let alone the magical oomph it be takin' to do that kinda spell." He gave a small shudder. "Death magic be a nasty business. Nobody be wantin' to get involved with that kind of bad mojo. Even the Fae that do, be tryin' to blame it on others so the reaper don' be lookin' for them."

Fan-fucking-tastic.

Mop was right. Death magic was a big no-no, and most Fae wouldn't even touch it. But there were some, the kind of Fae who had no qualms about using forbidden magics, and they always came with a price. Usually, that price was your life in return.

I could only hope I wasn't the one who was going to have to pay that price, since technically I had given the Shadows permission to use the magics. Just because I didn't do the spell, didn't mean I wasn't to blame.

"What be yer problem? Ye lookin' kind of sick."

My face must have shown my horror of the situation I had gotten myself in. Well, more like my human side had gotten myself in. If I'd had half the knowledge I did now about the Fae realm, I could have avoided so many problems that I found were creeping up on me. My insides twisted around in knots.

"I'm fine."

"No, ye ain't. Ye should sit down, yer not lookin' too good." Mop jumped up from his seat, holding a hand out to me.

"I'm fine, really." I tried to wave him off even as a spout of dizziness made me sway on my feet.

There was no use crying over what was and what could have been. It was the here and now that had me worried. What was going to happen to me? I didn't make a blood oath to the Shadows, not that I was sure it would have held, anyway. So I probably had a bit of time before I had to pay the debt. Hopefully, it was enough time to figure out how to get rid of the creepy smiling Shadow man. I had no ambitions to

48

be the Queen of the entire Fae Realm, let alone the Queen of the Shadow Realm.

Hell, I didn't even know if I wanted to be the Seelie Princess. They couldn't expect me to come crawling back so soon. I still had to get my own head sorted before I could rule anything, and I didn't even want to get started on my love life. Who the hell knew what was going on there? I knew I didn't.

I needed a vacation from my life, both of them. Where could I go where no one else would find me? Apparently, my mind had finally caught up with the shit storm that was my life and decided the floor looked like a lovely place to rest.

CHAPTER

4

GLAMOURED PAIN

AFTER MY EMBARRASSING fainting spell, I convinced Mop that the only thing I needed was to go to work. The quiet solace of the library was exactly where I needed to be. Here I could pretend I was just a normal girl trying to act like her boss wasn't a stone cold bitch and shelving books wasn't a tedious and suicide-inducing experience. But at least it was quiet.

Shoving the last book onto the shelf, I pushed my little cart around to the next aisle. Out of all the things I expected to be doing as a librarian, I actually thought shelving books would have been the most fun. Like I would discover a new adventure that I would have never learned had I not been trying to find the book that lived on that shelf. Instead, I found my hands felt grimy from some of the less cared for books, and my boss, Brandi, was constantly breathing down my neck.

She'd come to check on me at least five times since I had started shelving the latest intakes, and I was beginning to think she didn't trust me not to mess it up. Though, I had just feigned sick so I wouldn't have to come in after I got back from the Underground.

Could anyone blame a girl for not being up to facing the world with everything that had happened? I wouldn't.

Not that Brandi knew that. She took one look at my pale blonde hair and my vibrant blue eyes and pursed her lips like she wanted to blow her top off. But she hadn't said a word.

It was already two o'clock, and the most she had done was check up on me. Constantly. Of course, this made shelving all the more tedious.

When I picked the next book off my cart, I had a wild idea. I glanced around the aisle, peeking my head out between the bookshelves before turning back to the shelf in front of me.

I grinned down at the book in my hand— a hardback copy of some thriller that was all the rage—and tried to pull my magic up.

It kind of wiggled in my stomach, as if waking from sleep.

I hadn't tried to use my magic on purpose without being hurt or angry since the time at the glowing tree. I had gotten the fruit to float to me, but it had taken a bit of coaxing. It seemed like my magic was as prickly as I was and needed more than a little push to get moving.

It had to be like riding a bike. I used to be able to do all kinds of things with my magic without even thinking about it. One time, to get back at my Fae mother, I changed all the cherries in her tarts to raspberries, a flavor she finds completely vile, and I'd done it with just a snap of my fingers. Moving a book should be a piece of cake.

I stared down at the book in my hand, scrunching my brow together as if it would make me concentrate harder. The book twittered in my hands for a moment before floating just above my palms. Just as I was about to praise myself for my accomplishment, it dropped back into my hands. Startled by the sudden weight, my hands let the book slip through my fingers, and it landed with a loud boom on the library floor.

I winced, and then waited to hear the telltale sound of Brandi's feet, but she didn't make an appearance. I heaved a sigh of relief. Bending down to pick up the traitorous book, I dusted it off and grumbled under my breath at my own stupidity. Doing magic in public? Really? Did I want to be carted off to the mental ward? Or worse yet, experimented on? Because that was exactly what was going to happen if someone caught me.

I couldn't imagine the world reacting well to the thought of real magic. The human idea of magic was pyrotechnics and CGI. We couldn't even accept each other for our skin color or sexual orientation; the Fae mingling in this realm would be like an alien invasion, one that resulted in a shoot first and dissect later kind of war. Though, with the way things were going in the Underground, humans finding out about the Fae should be the last thing on my mind. Fae were disappearing and the Shadows were on the rampage.

"What are you doing, Katherine?" Brandi said from behind me.

I dropped the book mid-shelving. It slammed against the floor again, and I cringed. I drew back my shoulders and turned to face Brandi. Her lips were pursed so tight that I could barely make out the light pink of her lipstick. I couldn't tell if her eyebrows were raised or if the arch in them was just made that way. I stifled down a smile at the thought.

"I hope you are taking more care than this with the other books, Katherine. I wouldn't want to have to dock them from your pay for damages." The tone of her voice made me think that was exactly what she hoped to do.

My fists curled into tight balls, and I clenched my teeth. "No, we wouldn't want that."

She crossed her arms over her chest and appraised my ridged form. Oh, here it comes. I knew it would come sooner or later.

"You know, I don't know what I am going to do with you. First, I give you a job out of the kindness of my heart, even though you don't have the qualifications. Then not even three weeks in you call in sick supposedly with the flu, but then you come back with your hair colored completely blonde." She gestured a hand at my head. I had it pulled back into a ponytail to keep out of the way. "Not that I am complaining, mind you, it is a wonderful change from that garish auburn you've been sporting."

Each word was like an accelerant for my anger. She always knew how to give a backhanded compliment. I could feel my magic buzzing under my skin as she continued on about my looks.

"I could have forgiven the hair. I, myself, have skipped out on work to go on a much-needed spa day, but those eyes!" She pointed her perfectly manicured finger at me, and I forced myself not to step back as it got close to my face. "I don't know what kind of person wants to change the color of their eyes and to such an unnatural color. I didn't even know you wore contacts. Is that new? You know, you really should take better care of yourself. You're already not looking too fit." She paused, glancing down at my hips. "And we are getting older. We must keep up with our health, or what else do we have? Am I right?"

I tried to answer her—I really did—but I knew the moment I opened my mouth all of my magic would fly out of me and knock Brandi out of her thousand dollar heels, and then where would I be? Out of work and out of the Fae closet.

"Well?" She stared at me. "What do you have to say for yourself?"

Struggling to swallow my magic back down my throat, I made a gagging sound.

"Oh, my. You're not going to be sick are you?" Her face twisted in disgust.

A warm hand slid into mine, and a calm voice purred in my ear, "No, she won't. She will be just fine."

The feel of Chess' hand in mine calmed my magic, and it settled back into my skin where it belonged. The wide-eyed dreamy look in Brandi's eyes forced me to jerk around to look at Chess.

I almost didn't recognize him. He looked so normal—well, as normal as Chess could be as a hot runway model human. The cat ears were gone, and his pale pink hair was now a soft white that my fingers itched to be tangled in. He wore a dark button-down shirt with the top few buttons open to display the pale white skin below. He still had on an array of metal studded belts, but his tail was noticeably absent.

"Katherine? Who is your friend?" Brandi's voice pulled me away from Chess' emerald eyes that were alight with amusement.

"Uh. Um." I glanced at Brandi and then back to Chess, who graced me with a full, fangless grin. "He's um, my..."

Chess wrapped his arm around my waist and jerked me flush against his side. He slid his clawless finger under my chin and

56

tipped my face up to his, and in my speechless daze; I barely registered the feather-like brush of his lips across mine.

"Isn't it obvious? I'm Kat's beau."

I licked my lips at his words knowing I should protest, but I was too shocked to do much else but let him do what he willed.

"Oh? Her boyfriend? Really?" The incredulous tone of her voice snapped me out of my haze.

My eyes narrowed at the disbelieving raise of her brows, and I forced back a snarl. "Yes. My boyfriend."

Chess wasn't my anything, but I sure as hell wasn't letting that bitch know. She would dig her claws into him before I could say Wonderland. I wrapped my arms around Chess' waist and gave him a squeeze.

"Well hurry up and finish here. There is more work to do." She huffed and marched out of the aisle.

With the boss lady gone, I glanced up to ask Chess what the hell he was doing here but halted. His mouth was tight, and his eyes were slightly pinched. I moved back and looked him over more closely. His eyes, while as vibrant as ever in color, were filled with a bit of haze as if he weren't really there. His chest moved up and down in a rampant effort. I leaned away from him further and noticed a crimson wetness had shown up from where I had been pressed against him. His shirt stuck to him, and there was a slight stain of red on my own yellow shirt.

"Chess! You're bleeding."

"I'm fine, love." He pulled away from me and propped himself against one of the bookshelves, his image flickered back and forth between Fae and human form.

The pained sound of his voice did nothing to reassure me he was telling the truth. I stuck my head into the aisle checking for Brandi or any of my other coworkers. The library was pretty dead this time of day with school not out yet and parents still at work. I could probably get him to the bathroom undetected. With the way he was flickering, I didn't want to give some unsuspecting kiddie a scare.

"Come on." I grabbed Chess by the arm and dragged him out of the shelves and around the computers before ducking into the family bathroom.

Snapping the door shut behind me, I locked it and turned to Chess. He was resting against the sink, his fingers digging into the sides of the porcelain.

"What the fuck, Chess?" I stalked up behind him, trying to assess the damage from outside his clothes. "You get summoned to court for some unknown reason and come back bleeding?"

I pulled a handful of paper towels from the dispenser and lifted the side of his shirt to press them against his skin.

"You shouldn't bother, love." He grunted when I applied more pressure. "I'll heal on my own."

"That aside, you shouldn't be walking around when you are this hurt." I glared at him. "And since when could you use a glamour?"

"Why, because I'm a half-breed?" The venom in his voice knocked the complaint right out of me.

"No?" My voice became softer and less accusing than before. "I just assumed you'd have used it before now. I mean, if you were High Fae you would have."

"Like they are so great." He scoffed and then groaned as if the sound caused him pain. "I'll have you know, my mother was High Fae."

Curious now that he was actually opening up to me, I pressed more, "And your father?"

59

"Can't you guess?" He smirked at me with a grimace and then dropped his glamour to show his gorgeous pink mane in place of the pale blonde tresses. My eyes widened at the purpling bruise on his neck.

"Holy fuck." I stepped closer, putting one hand up to touch the bruise. He flinched, and I halted. "It's okay, Chess. I'm not going to hurt you, I just want to see."

He let out a pained chuckle and let me push his hair away from his throat to see the ring of purple blemishes around his neck. Being as careful as possible, I moved his collar aside. More bruises trailed down under his shirt.

I started to unbutton his shirt. I needed to see what else they had done to him. How much pain was he in?

"Woah, kitten." He brushed my hands away with a flirty grin. "If you wanted me out of my clothes, all you had to do was ask."

"Let me see, Chess."

His grin faltered. "What does it matter? I'm fine. The fiasco with your friend just opened them back up is all. They were almost done healing already."

"They?" I didn't ask this time. I grabbed the edges of his shirt and pulled. Buttons popped from the shirt and onto the floor, exposing his pale skin. I'd have liked to linger on the hard planes of his chest, but the dark array of bruises and small crisscross cuts that decorated his side drew my eyes.

"It's not bad at all. See?" He gestured to the area as he tried to hide a grimace on his face.

"Not bad at all?" I gaped at him. "Chess, you look like you've been in a fight with Teeth and lost!"

"Nonsense. Teeth wouldn't give me the time a day, let alone long enough to get in a fight with." He lifted up the edges of his shirt and frowned at the missing buttons. "You know, I really liked this shirt."

A growl left my throat. "Who did this to you?"

Not looking up from his shirt, he shrugged in a very feline way. "Oh, you know, the usual. An enraged spouse of some Fae or another upset that their loved one found their way into my loving claws."

I frowned. He was trying to deter me from the real culprit, but I didn't know him well enough to push the right buttons to get him to spill the beans. He, on the other hand, obviously knew what to do to rile me up.

61

"Never mind about me." He finally looked up from his shirt and locked his eyes on me. "You should be worrying about the mishap that almost happened out there."

"Everything is so hard now. I used to know this stuff. How to control it. It was unheard of for me to have something like that happen to me. So why can't I figure this out?" I bit my lip, frustration filling me.

He tapped me under the chin. "That's because your Fae body knew what to do. Your human body is still new to all this. You'll have to learn everything all over again, but this time without being able to ease into it like most Fae children do."

I poked my lip out in a pout. "How am I supposed to do that? Mop said only someone with powers like mine could help me."

"I will."

My ears perked up at that. "You could really help me? But you don't have the same abilities as me, do you?"

"Not all of them. But the basics would be enough to get you started. At least help keep you from creating a global incident." His tail slid out and wrapped itself around my waist. "And there is so much I want to teach you, my sweet Kat. Every one of them just as magical."

I tried not to grin at the corniness of his words, but there was something about him that always made me want to smile or rip off his clothes. While the latter had potential, he was right: my almost blowing up on Brandi was more important at the moment than the bruises that would fade. If only the ache in my heart that said something wasn't right would fade with it.

CHAPTER 5

SCHOOL OF MAGIC

AFTER WORK I found myself standing in the backyard of my grandmother's house with Chess ready to take on the role of teacher.

"Glamours are the basic level magic that many High Fae children master before their first five years. You remember this, correct?" His eyes trailed over me.

Even in my baggiest shirt and most unflattering sweatpants, I still felt like his eyes were undressing me. Too bad my insides didn't find that a bad thing. Reeling back my hormones, I focused on what he asked me.

"Yeah." I shuffled from one foot to the other, recalling what I knew of glamours. I remembered being able to use it in my previous life, but Alice and Chess were the only ones I'd seen use one as a human.

"Well? Don't keep teacher waiting," Chess drawled, which ended up sounding more like a purr.

I crossed my arms over my chest and leveled him with an unamused glare. "There are three kinds of glamours."

"Right you are, and what are they?" He held up three fingers.

I threw my hands up in the air with a sigh, giving into his silly game. "Well, there's a visual glamour."

Chess smirked at my unenthused answer. "And that is?"

The fucker was enjoying this.

"A visual glamour only makes you look like whatever you are changing into." Before he could jump in and ask another asinine question, I continued, "Say you are really fat and want to appear thinner, it doesn't mean you are thinner. Someone that tries to hug you is going to freak out when they get stopped by your big invisible belly."

He gave me a disapproving look at my analogy but then curled his lips into a teasing grin. "So, what if you wanted to look and feel thinner? Not that you need it." He took a step closer to me and placed his hands on the swell of my hips. "Curves like yours keep men up at night."

I snorted at his attempt to flirt and pushed him away, holding up two fingers. "Second kind. Physical glamour. The ability to not only look but feel like what you are trying to pretend to be."

"And what's left? You can look and feel like anyone. Why would you need to go a step further?" He leaned into me, unconvincingly sniffing me as a hint and not for his own perverse pleasure.

"Because Fae have a great sense of smell, which makes it harder to lie to them, so you would need to not only change your appearance but change your scent too." I tapped my chin as I thought about it. "It's actually something that is really difficult to do and takes a lot of magic and control to accomplish, but if a Fae happens to be able to do it, they could fool even the most powerful Fae into believing they were someone else."

As the words left my mouth, I realized something. I'd been trying to figure out how Alice had been able to trick Dorian into believing she was me. It hadn't even crossed my mind that she could have done a full glamour because it was so unheard of that it wasn't even something that was considered anymore. It was the only logical reason that Dorian could have been tricked, and if it was true, I owed Dorian a huge apology. But why did I see Alice when he saw me? It didn't make any sense, unless Alice was better at controlling her glamour than she thought.

If Alice really had that kind of power, she was as much of a threat as the Shadow man, if not more. And if the Shadow man got ahold of Alice? We were all in trouble.

"What are you thinking about in that pretty little head of yours?" Chess asked with a hint of concern.

My gaze jerked up to him. I took a startled step back at how close his face was to mine. The green in his eyes gleamed with curiosity.

"Uh, nothing," I muttered, but it didn't sound convincing even to me.

He frowned at my lie but didn't question it. Instead, he strolled away from me and into the lines of vegetables in the garden. My gaze wandered after him, watching the way his pants clung to his behind. Thankfully, he had left the glamour off since we were at the house. I didn't expect any company anytime soon, and if anyone did choose to stop by, I hoped being in the backyard would give us enough warning to be prepared.

When he was done doing his little catwalk and made his way back over to me, the frown was gone from his face and in its place, his usual flirty smile. I was beginning to think that smile wasn't meant to seduce but to hide his real feelings. It made me wonder what else he concealed behind that smile.

"So, you know what a glamour is. Now to put it into effect." He flipped his braided hair over his shoulder, a movement I started to dissect to have some kind of secret meaning as well.

"Okay?" I let the question hang in the air.

Instead of answering, he reached around and pulled my hair out of my messy bun, and when he brushed my hair out with his fingers, I resisted the urge to purr. He lifted one of the pale strands up to his nose, his eyes watching my face.

"Okay." I cleared my throat, angling my head to pull my hair from his grip. "So you want me to glamour my hair?"

Straightening up, he gave a nonchalant shrug. "Unless you would like to keep explaining your appearance to your friends and family."

"Well, my hair isn't so hard to explain. Lots of people color their hair nowadays, and no one really cares. What I really need to glamour are my eyes. Telling Brandi that I got colored contacts is one thing, but I don't want to have to constantly defend it to my mother, which I'm sure will happen when I eventually can't avoid her any longer."

"If you insist. Now focus," he demanded.

My brow creased, but I closed my eyes and tried to focus on changing the color of my irises. I felt a bit silly closing my eyes. Before, I didn't even need to think about my magic to make what I wanted happen, but as every bad martial artist movie taught me, nothing gets you focused like losing one of your senses. All I was missing was a training montage and Chess singing a fatherly ballad about letting me find my way. Though, the thought of calling Chess *daddy* in any sense was a little too on the kinky side for my tastes.

Taking a deep breath, I reached for the magic inside me, coaxing it up to do my will. It fluttered around; slow and languid at first before creeping up to greet me. I felt it fill me up like a pressure under my skin.

Next, I tried to imagine what my eyes looked like before: a deep forest green with a bit of gold around the middle, almost more hazel than green. With the image in my mind, I pushed my magic, willing my eyes to be that color again. My eyes tingled, and then the magic became dormant once more.

Peeking an eye open, I chanced a look at Chess, who cocked his head.

"Well? Did I do it?" I strained my eyelids open so he could see.

A deep frown filled his face as he assessed the change I couldn't see. "Not exactly."

"What do you mean, not exactly? Either I did, or I didn't." I gave an impatient huff.

"Well, you changed them all right, but unless your eyes were a muddy kind of vomit color, I think you need more practice." He tapped his chin in thought before stepping up to me. "I have an idea."

I hesitated at his close proximity and went to take a step back but was stopped by his hand on my wrist.

"Wait. Hear me out before you start getting suspicious. I'm not going to bite you." He gave me a cheeky grin. "Well, at least not right now."

"Like that makes it any better," I grumbled, but let him draw me closer.

"I think what your problem is, is imagination." He placed both of his hands on my face, bringing me eye to eye with him. "We should have started with this to begin with, rather than making you rely on your shotty human memory."

"Hey!" I pulled back but didn't get far with my face trapped between his claws. "My memory is fine."

He gave an indelicate snort. "So I see."

"Fine." I crossed my arms over my chest. "What do you want me to do, all masterful one?"

A dark heated look filled his eyes. I swallowed hard, an apology on my lips, but he shrugged.

"You are going to make your eyes look like mine."

My shoulders slumped with relief that he wasn't going to make a big deal about my attitude.

"No offense," I said. "But I don't exactly think having cat eyes will help my little situation."

He gave me a pointed look, and I clammed up any further protests.

"The point is that you will have something in front of you to visualize and not rely on your own mind to create it. This is just step one. Once you can copy my eyes, you can go back to working on your normal color. All right?"

My lips curled down. I didn't really like his plan, but I shrugged in acceptance anyway.

"So what I want you to do is focus on my eyes." His pupils locked on mine.

"But don't I need to wake my magic first?" I tried to pull back to look at him properly.

"No. Don't even think about your magic. Just watch here." He pulled my face closer to him until our noses brushed against each other.

I glanced down to his mouth, so close to mine, and my tongue dipped out to wet my suddenly dry lips. As much as I liked to berate Chess for his lecherous ways, I remembered what it was like to be at the mercy of those lips. The way he kissed me made me feel like he wasn't just trying to taste me, but devour me. As if he couldn't get enough. And his hands could do the most wicked things. He didn't even have to touch the usual places that got me going with most guys. His hands on my skin were enough.

"Focus, Kat." His voice came out a rough growl as if he too was affected by our closeness. "Focus on my eyes. On the color. The emerald green that sparkles in the sun at the right angle. The little details. The different shades that make up the color as a whole." The soothing sound of his voice in correspondence to looking deep into his eyes made the rest of the world melt away until it was just him. "Do you see the way the pupil dilates as the clouds pass over the sun?"

I hummed in my throat a response. I felt like a snake trapped in a charmer's song. Except this charmer's body was far more lethal and his voice more tempting than any flute could provide.

"You want to have eyes like these. Of course you do. It is only normal to want what others have," he whispered the words like the little devil on my shoulder telling me it was all right to want the naughty things. In fact, he would help me get them. "Tell me, my little kitty Kat. Tell me you want them."

I only gaped at him in a daze before I realized I did want his eyes. I wanted to be able to see what he saw. Look out at the world from his point of view and see how it would feel to be Cheshire S. Cat: sexy, confident, a bit cocky, and dangerous to not only my libido but my heart as well.

"Tell me?" He asked again, his voice becoming huskier as if knowing exactly what was running through my mind.

"I do," I croaked out before clearing my throat to try again. "I want them."

"Then let yourself have them." Without warning, his lips crashed onto mine.

My mouth opened in a startled gasp and his tongue swept into my mouth. His hands moved from the side of my face to the back of my neck, tilting me to a more pleasing angle. I let myself be controlled by our desire. My hands sought out the front of his shirt as my magic spread through me like a tidal wave with one goal in mind: to give me what I wanted.

My body hummed with power, and it poured into every inch of me. My senses became more aware of my surroundings. The feel of the cotton shirt beneath my fingers almost burned the tips from its roughness. My hands moved away to tangle in the softest of silk strands at his shoulders. I stroked them as my nose became engulfed in his deep, masculine smell. The combination of his scent mixed with the delicious taste of his lips caused my insides to clench in a consuming need.

"What the hell be goin' on here?" Mop's voice cut through the fog of lust and magic muddling my brain.

I jerked back from Chess, a sharp pain stinging my tongue. The coppery taste of blood filled my mouth.

"Shit." The curse word came out of my mouth but was not in my voice. It was deeper and buttery. I glanced over at Chess who gave an amused, but slightly surprised smile, not at all comforting my fears.

I reached a hand up to touch where my lip had gotten nicked by my — fangs? I had fangs? My heart sped up as I spread my fingers out to touch my face. Gone were the soft rounded edges, and in their place were more defined cheekbones and a strong jawline.

Holy fuck! I chanted over and over in my head as I took in each changed feature.

My eyes had become more sensitive to the light, and I squinted as I looked down at my body. My clothes were still the same, but my baggy sweatpants were tight against my body as was the t-shirt, showing off my new defined muscles. I was half tempted to check down my pants to see what was going on down there as well, but Mop's voice broke my thoughts.

"Is one of ye goin' to tell me what is goin' on? Why be there two of ye? And where be Lady?" Mop waved his hands at us.

"Yes, yes. Trip wishes to know, Trip does." Trip popped in.

His beady eyes seemed huge against his furred face as he stood up on the tips of his feet to get a better look at me. His ears were pointed high up in the air, and his tail wagged behind him.

Chess smirked and gestured his hand at me. Mop and Trip turned their gaze to where I stood. I tugged on my new pink hair, feeling weird and uncomfortable in Chess' skin. After a moment, I gave a nervous laugh and waved.

"Hi, guys." The buttery smooth sound of Chess' voice coming out of my own mouth sounded awkward and not sexy at all. How did he do it?

"Lady?" Trip eyed me for a moment, before creeping up to me, his nose pointed toward me to sniff the air. "Lady looks like Smiling Cat, Lady does. Lady even smells like Smiling Cat!"

Mop circled around me, one hand stroking his chin as he took in my appearance. "How be this possible?"

I gave an inelegant shrug. Geez, how did he make his body move so fluidly, so sensual? While I might look like the feline, I sure as hell didn't feel like him. It was like a square that had been shoved into a circle peg. Cramped and claustrophobic. I was beginning to feel a bit light headed.

A coppery metal smell filled my senses, and a warm trickle came out of my nose. Chess' nose. Somebody's nose. My hand went up to touch where I had started bleeding when the world tilted.

Strong arms wrapped around me, breaking my fall, and the musky scent that was purely Chess mixed with the coppery smell of blood. My limbs felt heavy, and my eyelids fought to stay open as my magic flowed out of me, leaving me empty and weak inside.

"Don't worry love, I've got you." Chess lifted me into his arms and carried me across the yard.

As the door to the kitchen closed behind us, I lost consciousness.

CHAPTER 6

DEBTS TO BE PAID

WHEN I AWOKE, I found myself lying in my own bed. I jerked up and then grabbed my head in pain. *Fuck.* It was like a horde of sorority girls were jumping around having a pillow fight on every squishy surface of my brain.

"Slow now, kitten," Chess said from somewhere nearby. I peeked out from my partially closed eyes to see him leaning against the doorframe of my bedroom. "You're going to feel a bit worn out for a while."

"What happened?" Before he could answer, I remembered. "Wait!" I glanced down at myself, and if my head didn't throb so much, I would have jumped up and done a little dance. "I'm me again!"

I wrapped my arms around myself in a tight hug, not caring that Chess was laughing at me. I touched my face, stroking the soft curve of my cheek, and gave a blissful sigh.

"Should I leave you two alone?" Chess chuckled as he made his way over to the bed. "Though, I'd be lying if I said I didn't want to stay and watch."

I was too happy to be myself again to chastise him for being such a perv. I plopped back against the headboard and sighed. I never wanted to experience that again. I couldn't even imagine what it had looked like to Mop and Trip seeing Chess making out with himself. I was embarrassed to find out parts of me heated at the vision of two Chesses.

And I thought he was perverted.

Shaking my head, I turned back to him, ignoring the knowing grin on his face. "So what happened? How did I even do that?"

He hummed to himself and leaned onto one arm. "You weren't able to do a full glamour before?"

"No, I think I would remember being able to completely glamour myself." I had a few abilities back when I was full Fae, but nothing that powerful. I could manipulate objects, and I had a super green thumb—I could just touch a dying plant and bring new life to it—but I wasn't about to win any magical awards for it.

"Well, it must have something to do with your human side." Chess offered while one of his fingers traced circles on my thigh over the covers.

I placed my hand on his to stop him, but it only caused a tingle to rush through me. I moved his hand out of my lap and drew my legs up to my chest. Placing my chin on my knees, I looked off to the side and ignored his knowing grin.

"I'm not sure. I would think being mostly human would make me, weaker not stronger," I said.

"Not necessarily. Magic doesn't have the kind of rules you would think."

I snorted. "But the Fae are all about the rules."

"True, but that is self-inflicted." He waved his hand in the air. "If we didn't give ourselves restrictions, then there would be chaos. Fae killing one another. Jumping time with no regards for the consequences. You never know what could happen."

Guilt filled me when he mentioned jumping time. That guy. J. S., whoever he was, was dead because of me. Because of what I let the Shadows do.

80

"The cat be right." Mop waddled into my room, Trip hopping along behind him. "There be rules that be there for a reason."

"I don't remember there being so many rules before."

Trip jumped up onto my bed, bouncing on the spring mattress. A slight sound of joy came out of his mouth. I let out a small giggle at the happiness on his face. It had only been about a week, but I'd missed Trip and his childlike personality. He made everything seem fun and new. If only everyone was that way.

"Trip is happy to see Lady is Lady again, Trip is." The opalaught snuggled up next to me on the bed, clinging to my arm. I stroked between his ears and smiled.

"I'm glad to be me again too, and I'm really glad to see you." I squeezed him tight. His ears tickled my face. "How is Hare holding up?"

Trip's ears dropped at the mention of Hare, and I regretted saying anything. "Hare is no good. Hare is not."

"Why? What happened?"

"It be them damn Shadows!" Mop cursed and spit on the ground. I grimaced, not looking forward to cleaning up brownie slobber. "Hare be gone missin' and Hatter be beside himself. He has locked himself inside his home and won't come out. Most of the other Fae have done the same. Bunch of cowards!"

"You'd be cowering in your home if you'd met the Shadow man too," I growled out then quickly tried to change the subject when I realized my mistake. "So, why are you two here?"

Trip opened his mouth but was interrupted by Mop.

"How do ye know what it be like? I only just told ye they be corporeal the other day." The suspicion in Mop's eyes cut through me like a razor.

I looked away and out toward the mirror in my room. It was one of those long, full-length mirrors. Ever since I got back I had taken up the habit of covering it with a dark sheet. I could never be too careful of who was listening.

"You remember how I said I took care of it?" I started, still not meeting any of their eyes.

"Yeah?" Mop asked.

There was a lot of judgment just in that one word. I couldn't imagine how the grumpy brownie was going to react when he heard what I had done.

"Well, you know I let Alice out, right?"

Mop nodded at me.

"And how I had a run in with the Shadows while in there?"

"Ye still never told me why ye hair turned white, though now knowin' what I know now, I'd imagine it be havin' more to do with yer Fae powers than thems Shadows."

"Actually, that was partly Seer's fault," I pointed out. "Just ask the prince. He was there."

"But what happened with the Shadows, kitten?" Chess leaned in closer, a wicked glint in his eye as if he had more at stake with what I had to say than any of them.

"Uh." I hesitated. "Well, you see. What happened is..." I took a deep breath and then just spilled it all out in one go. "They want me to be their queen so they can get back at the other Queens, but they wouldn't let me wake up so I could find Alice 'cause of the whole incorporeal thing, and so we made a deal where they could take the body of one of the Fae locked away in the Hall of Mirrors that was going to die soon anyway. Except, they kind of stretched the truth on that one, and now they are running amuck, and it's all my fault 'cause they are just looking for me!"

I heaved in air as I tried to catch my breath. I watched the faces of those around me, waiting for the horror and anger that

83

was sure to creep onto their faces, but they all busted out laughing.

"What? What's so funny?" I growled out. How could they find this amusing?

I searched Mop's face, but he just slapped his knee as his laughter became worse. Trip rolled around on the bed, giggling like a madman, and even Chess, who was supposed to be on my side, was chuckling at my expense.

"Would someone tell me what is going on?" I twisted my fists into the sheets of my bed, trying to get a hold on my anger. I didn't remember being so emotional before, but for some reason the more magic I used, the more it grew, the more of an emotional wreck I became.

Chess quit laughing first and patted me on the knee. "We aren't laughing at you, precious."

"Then what are you laughing at?" I pouted and crossed my arms over my chest.

"The Shadows—" Mop tried to get out but started chortling again. "Sorry, sorry." He coughed, forcing his laughter back though his eyes still glittered with unshed tears. "I be fine now."

I raised my eyebrow. "Well?"

"The Shadows don't be needin' ye to get their revenge." The smirk on Mop's face looked out of place. "They can be gettin' their own revenge without ye helpin' them."

"Is that so? Then why were they trying so hard to get me on their side? They said they needed someone who wasn't bound by the same rules as they were and obviously that means me." I didn't know why I was trying to justify why the Shadow man would want me. It wasn't like I had any intention of going over to the dark side, so to speak, but to hear Mop say that I didn't matter kind of stung.

Mop exchanged a look with Trip and Chess as if wondering what he should say.

"What? What are you guys hiding from me?" I glanced at Chess, betrayal clear on my face. I trusted him to tell me the truth at least. Though, I shouldn't be surprised he was keeping things from me— he was a cat, after all. Who the hell knew what was going on in a feline's mind?

"Well, while you are quite a catch, my dear, and any Fae would be lucky to have you," Chess said, picking my hand up and stroking it, "You aren't exactly the only one."

"What do you mean?" I ignored the way his hand made my skin tingle with every touch.

"What the cat be tryin' to tell ye," Mop jumped in, "is ye ain't the only one who be able to pass between worlds without a key."

"Well, I know that. Chess is half and half, and he can too." I had a sudden thought, and my attention snapped to him. "Is that who hurt you? Was the Shadow man trying to get you to help him?"

Chess exchanged a look with Mop but didn't answer. Instead, Trip tugged on a strand of my once again blonde hair.

"Lady is right, Lady is. Smiling Cat can, but so can others, they can." Trip gave me a small, sad smile as if he knew something that I didn't, which it seemed like that was going on a lot lately.

"What others?" I asked, but they once again looked amongst themselves. I'd had enough. "Stop doing that. Stop acting like I'm a child that needs protecting. I'm older than all of you combined. Well, my soul is at least, but that's beside the point" I waved a finger in each of their direction. "You are keeping stuff from me, and I want—no, I need—to know what it is."

Chess gave me a sympathetic half smile and then let out a reluctant sigh. "You have to remember that a lot has happened in the time you were gone. Not all of it good."

Mop snorted. "That be an understatement if I ever heard one."

Chess snapped his eyes to Mop in warning. Mop crossed his arms and stared Chess down as if daring him to chastise him.

"Like I was saying," Chess turned back to me, ignoring the defiant little man, "A lot has happened in the time since you died and now."

"I know that, and I know there is a lot of catching up to do, and if I'm going to make a sound decision on where my place in the world is—any world—shouldn't I have all the facts?"

"Sometimes the truth isn't always good for you," Chess warned.

"I don't care. I want to know," I urged, but none of them offered up an explanation. I opened my mouth to continue to argue when Trip tugged on my arm.

"Lady can't ask friends that, Lady can't. There are rules, there are." Trip's frown did nothing to ease my need to know. In fact, it just made it stronger. They were hiding something. They all were.

"Even you, Chess? I thought you didn't have to obey the rules?" I quirked a brow at him.

He looked me dead in the eye with a serious glare.

"This one I do. Let's have no more talk of it." The strictness in his voice called for no argument, but his face soon changed to a curious, playful manner as he turned to Trip. "What are you two doing here, anyway? Did his highness not trust me to keep our princess safe?"

"Bah! Like his highness would be askin' us? I be here deliverin' a message. A reminder." Mop's dark eyes locked with mine.

"A reminder?"

"That ye made promises. Blood oaths. Oaths ye better be keepin' if ye know what be good for ya."

Oh. That oath.

"Teeth be gettin' impatient. Ye haven' fulfilled your end of ye bargain yet. Ye don't be havin' much time left, can't ye feel it?" Mop wagged his finger at me.

This was another one of those instances where I was supposed to feel something and I didn't. When I had made the deal with the big fuzzy wall with sharp teeth that had become his namesake, I was supposed to have felt some kind of magical power in my blood. But like many things that had changed about me, the human half of me seemed to negate any rules that came from being Fae. So technically there wouldn't be any consequences, but the honorable part of me urged me to do the right thing.

I smacked my head back against my headboard with a groan and then blew out a hard breath.

"Fine, let's get this over with." I nudged Chess over to get out of the bed and moved to the edge.

"Are you sure you are all right now, love?" Chess held his hand out to me with concern in his eyes.

I nodded, placing my hand in his. My head had stopped throbbing, and the weak feeling I had was gone.

The promise I had made to make biscuits for Teeth in exchange for my passage flashed through my mind. A hundred biscuits were nothing in the human world. Besides, it wasn't like I was making biscuits from scratch. Who even did that anymore?

"Oh! Oh! Can Trip help, can Trip?" He jumped up and down on my bed his tail wagging behind him.

"Sure you can, Trip." I smiled back at him and headed for the bedroom door.

My room wasn't big, but then again, I didn't have many belongings, so I didn't need much. A stand-up dresser, single door closet, and a queen sized bed. The bedroom was my grandmother's, which was easily identified by the large flower print on the comforter and the massive amount of throw pillows. Really, who needed that many pillows? They were just there for looks, anyway.

"A hundred biscuits be a large order," Mop stated as he followed me into the kitchen. "How ye goin' to make all thems biscuits on ye own?"

I smirked at Mop and opened the fridge where I had bought ten containers of biscuit dough.

I grabbed one of the cylinders and held it out to him. "Like this."

"What be that?" Mop gave the tub a cautious but curious once-over.

"Biscuits." I smacked the end of the cylinder on the side of the counter, and the container popped open.

Pushing a chair over to the counter, Mop glanced over my shoulder as I began to lay out the little white circles onto a pan.

"Thems ain't biscuits." He poked his finger at the dough, and then sniffed his finger with a grimace.

I gave an impatient sigh. "Not yet they aren't, but in about ten minutes they will be." I moved over to the oven and hit the preheat button. "Humans might not have magic, but they have their own form of instant gratification."

Mop frowned. "I don't know. Seems like cheatin' to me."

I shoved the pan into the oven and closed it with a smack. "It's not cheating, it's efficient. I don't have hours to be slaving away in the kitchen to make some stupid biscuits. This way is faster, and Teeth won't even know the difference." I turned to the Fae in the room. "I thought you would know all about modern wonders?"

"Not everyone that comes to the human realm actually ventures out into the populated areas," Chess said from where he lounged at the kitchen table. He tapped his claws on the wood.

"So, you guys just come into our world to hang out in the woods and occasionally steal from people's gardens? That makes no sense whatsoever." I shook my head at Trip who was nodding in an excessive manner.

"Trip likes Lady's carrots, Trip does!"

I smiled at the opalaught, because really, what else could I do? He was just too cute. But I expected more from Mop.

"What about you?"

Mop plopped down in the chair he was standing on and scoffed. "Like I want to be here? I only be here for Trip. I have me own family to worry 'bout. I don' be needin' no human rubbish. Me wife would be havin' me by the goods if I brought any of that silly stuff home."

"You have a wife?" I didn't try to hide the surprise in my voice. Not too long ago, Mop was complaining about the Seelie calling him ugly. That didn't sound like someone who was in a happy and healthy marriage.

"Yeah. What about it?" He crossed his arms over his chest. "Do ye think I can't get a woman? I have ye know, I be a catch amongst brownies. Any Fae or human would be lucky to have me."

"Mop is right, Mop is." Trip nodded. "Mop has biggest house in the whole brownie village, Mop does. Though, Mop's wife isn't very nice, she's not."

"Trip!" Mop shot him a glare.

Trip pulled his ears down around his face in defense against Mop's sharp tone. I opened my mouth to comment when the oven went off at the same time the front door slammed shut, and the worst sound in the world called out from the living room.

92

CHAPTER 7

MOTHER KNOWS BEST

MY MOTHER. THE sound of her voice struck fear in the very heart of any socialite who dared to cross her.

My human mother, who didn't know anything about the Fae realm, or that I wasn't completely human, had arrived home. If she stepped into the kitchen right now, she would see a little brown man whose head was not shaped right to be a normal human, a rabbit that could be rabid if tempted the wrong way, and a male supermodel who looked like he just stepped out of a Japanese comic book.

Yeah. That would go over well.

"Katherine! Did you hear me?" her voice called out from the living room. "It is rude not to greet your guests at the door."

"You're not a guest, Mom," I shouted and then turned to the others. "Hurry out the back door before she sees you. I'll leave the biscuits out on the counter for you to take to Teeth."

I pointed at Chess to tell him to throw his glamour on or get out, but he had beat me to the punch and sat with an amused, but curious expression on his face.

The back door slammed shut just as my mother stepped into the kitchen, marking Mop and Trip's exit. I proceeded to pull the biscuits out of the oven, knowing the rant that was about to come.

"Are you listening to me, Katherine? I swear you are just like your father, so defiant. Far too much spirit for a proper young lady." My mother slipped off her white gloves and held them in one hand.

She, who had barely hit fifty, was all about the Hillary Clinton look: matching skirt and blazers in sensible colors that didn't scream harlot, and enough hairspray in her hair to open a new hole in the ozone layer. She could have gone the hot trophy wife way, but instead, she went the 'I have to be the head of every charity and restoration group in the county' way. My dad might be a bookworm, and know how to crunch numbers like nobody's business, but my mother knew exactly how to wheedle the most out of her wealthiest investors.

Leaning back against the counter, I waited to see how long she would ream into me before she even noticed Chess was in the room. It could be a while. When she got on a tangent, there really was no stopping her.

"And your hair." She waved her gloves at me, a scowl on her face. "While I appreciate that you have finally gone to the length to get it colored, I really wish you would have called me. I would have gotten you in with my girl." She primped the edges of her own stiff, blonde bob. "And I'm not so sure I like the blonde on you. Your sister can pull it off because she has the right skin tone, but sadly, you take after your father in that aspect. You might consider going more of a Champagne blonde next time. I can..." she trailed off mid rant when Chess couldn't hold back a chuckle.

"Well, hello. Katherine, why didn't you tell me you had company?" Her blue eyes stabbed into me, showing her displeasure in a nonverbal capacity. She was good like that. A single look from her could kill a guy's boner in an instant and a young daughter's self-esteem for life. My mother turned to Chess with a smile. "I don't believe we've met. I'm Katherine's mother, Sylvia."

Chess unwrapped himself from his chair and took my mother's hand in his, bending down to brush his lips on top of it.

"It is a pleasure to meet such a lovely woman," he purred, humor lighting his eyes as he looked up at my mother through his long eyelashes. The cheater. "I can see where my Kat gets her good looks from."

My mother giggled. The stiff upper lipped Republican fucking giggled. Like a high school girl! Well, at least I wasn't the only one affected by Chess' charm.

"Why, I don't know about that, but you are charming." She giggled again, and I found myself smirking at them.

"Mom, this is Chess. Chess, my mom." I watched with ongoing amusement as I introduced them.

At least Chess was good for something other than eye candy. I might have to make him my certified mother-daughter buffer.

"Chess?" She looked at me in question. "That's an unusual name. However, did you come by it?"

"It's a family name." Chess took the inquiry in stride. "My full name is Cheshire, but as you may notice my friends call me Chess, as may you."

"So, is that what you two are? Friends?" She placed an innocent hand up to her face, looking between us.

"Mom!"

My mother, ever the tactful one.

Chess chuckled in that way that made my insides tingle. He left my mother's side and approached me. Wrapping a strand of my hair around his finger, he tugged on it, sending a small zing into my scalp.

"I would like to know as well." Chess' eyes lit up with humor. "Are we friends, pet?"

My face became hot at the nickname, and his proximity only made my embarrassment worse under my mother's watchful eye.

"Yes," I stuttered, not exactly sure what we were.

I was attracted to him, but my life was way too complicated to be thinking about having a boyfriend, human or not. There was also the ever-looming question of what to do about Dorian haunting me every moment of my life.

"Yes? Yes, what?" Chess prodded.

I glared up at him and gritted my teeth, no longer amused. "Yes, we are friends."

My mother made a knowing hum.

My eyes snapped back to her. "What?"

She looked down as she began to put her gloves back on. "Oh, nothing. I can see you are very good friends. But I really should be going, dear. I only came by to see if you were coming to Sunday dinner, since you missed the last one."

"And you couldn't have called for that?" I patted my pocket, wondering where the hell my phone had gone. I swear I had it a moment ago. Maybe it was still in the backyard.

"I would have if you bothered to answer any of my calls." She frowned briefly before turning to Chess with a smile. "It was delightful to meet you, Chess. I do hope to see you again soon. Maybe you could come with Katherine to Sunday dinner? Then you could meet the whole family. It's been awhile since Katherine has brought any of her friends over to meet us." She gave me a pointed look.

"No," I jumped in before Chess could answer. "No. I'm sure Chess has other places to be, other business to attend to than a silly family dinner."

"I'd be delighted," Chess called out over my head, and I glared up at him.

"Good," my mother chirped. "Well, now that is settled, Katherine, will you walk me to the door?"

"Of course, Mom," I gritted out and followed her out of the kitchen, knowing that Chess was enjoying himself far too much.

When we reached the front door, she pounced.

"What is going on with you? You don't answer any of our calls. Your father is beside himself with worry, and you know how he gets. His cholesterol is already through the roof, and he doesn't need to be overstressing himself."

I sighed and grabbed my hair. "I'm sorry. I'm just going through some stuff right now. I didn't mean to make Dad worry."

"Stuff like missing work?"

"Ugh. What? Did Brandi call you? That's why you came by?" I growled, hating that bitch all the more.

"And what about your sudden hair change. Or maybe your unusual need for colored contacts? Are you insecure?" She brushed a strand of hair away from my face and tucked it behind my ear in the only motherly manner she had ever portrayed to me. "Did someone say something to you, Katherine? Because you know, I always say that no one can make you feel bad, only you can."

"I know, Mom. God. If anyone makes me feel insecure, it is your and Linda's constant pestering." I pushed her hand away. "You better go easy on Chess. I don't want this to end up like what happened with my prom date."

"I don't know what you mean." My mother sniffed.

"I mean it." I pointed a finger at her. "We aren't dating, so get that thought out of your head. I will not have you interrogating him. He is just a friend."

My mother smirked. "Well, if all of your friends look at you the way that delicious male specimen does, then you have been holding out on your old mother. Why if I was ten years younger, I'd—"

"Ew. Mom, really? TMI." My mouth twisted in disgust.

"Well, you can be safe and assured that there will be no interrogation," she continued, opening the front door. "I'll leave you to your friend then. I'll see you on Sunday."

"Bye, Mom." I rolled my eyes and closed the door tight behind her.

"Well, that was entertaining," Chess purred from the kitchen door.

"For you, maybe." I threw myself on the couch and covered my eyes with my arm. "I'd rather have a root canal without the numbing agent."

The couch shifted beside me as Chess sat down next to me. I let my arm fall to give him a curious look. He had dropped the glamour as soon as my mother had left, and his tail was whipping back and forth like it had something it needed to get out.

"Yes?"

"What is your family like?"

I leaned my head back against the couch and shrugged. "You know, like any other family. My sister is a pain, has always been Miss Perfect, so, of course, I get compared to her in every way."

"Perfect?" He arched his brow, leaning into me. "I don't know how she could ever be more perfect than you."

"Hold on, Romeo." I gave an uncomfortable chuckle.

"Romeo?" He cocked his head to the side.

Oh, right. He probably had never heard of Shakespeare or any other references from the human world.

"Never mind." I shook my head. "Anyway, my dad's great. He's what the business world calls a fixer. He goes into a company that is sinking and crunches the numbers until he comes up with a plan that pulls them out of hot water and into the Fortune 500." I glanced at Chess. He nodded in a polite manner. I frowned. God, I was lame. "He's my best friend," I finished, trying to pull the conversation out of the snooze zone. "And, my mom, well, you met her." I chuckled in an apologetic manner.

"They sound wonderful," Chess said absently as he played with the ends of my hair.

"What about you?" I moved away, drawing his gaze up to me. "What's your family like?"

At that moment, something passed in his eyes, dark and a bit sad, before a lopsided grin covered his face. "Same as any other family, I suppose. But more importantly..." he paused for emphasis. "About this friend thing."

His fingers found their way back into my hair.

"Yeah. What about it?" I closed my eyes and tried not to moan at the way his digits massaged my scalp. If he kept doing that, he might very well move up from friend to Master of Kat.

"Does it come with any perks?"

"Perks?" I popped an eye open to look at him. "What kind of perks?"

He gave me a sultry smirk and tugged me closer. "The friendly kind."

I squeaked out, 'Oh!' and then his mouth covered mine. Unlike his other kisses, which were meant to seduce and consume, this one seemed more like he was trying to lose himself in me. As if talking about his family made him need reassurance that he was really there and he was all right. I told myself that was why I let him kiss me. That the reason I dug my fingers into his hair and pulled him closer was because he needed this, not because I did.

He groaned and cupped my hip to bring me closer. He kept his hands on my waist, not creeping up or down, as he was perfectly content to continue ravishing my mouth in slow and sure movements. It was different but mildly unsatisfying.

The part of me that had given in and decided this was a good idea, that we wanted—no, needed—this, wasn't happy with the gentle nips and sliding of our mouths together. It needed more. I arched my back to try to get him to take the hint, but he only held my face in his hand, changing the angle of our kiss so as not to nick my tongue on his teeth.

Growling in frustration, I took matters into my own hands. I used my weight to push back against him until I was leaning over him and then threw one leg onto the other side of him. Sitting astride his lap, I could feel every inch of him pressed between my legs. My hands tightened on his hair so I could get just a bit closer.

He moved his hands down to my hips, pressing me down against him as if knowing just what I needed from him. When he began to move my hips back and forth against his, he pulled his mouth away from mine. My eyes fluttered open and met his as small zings where our hips touched moved through me.

When I couldn't seem to get the right amount of friction, my hand went to the waist of his pants. Just as my hands found the skin of his stomach underneath his shirt, a throat cleared behind me. I froze in place. With my hands still on Chess' delectable abs, I looked over my shoulder to see Mop's disapproving frown.

I moved to get up, but he held up his hands. "Oh no, don't be stoppin' on me account. I just be here to let the cat know they be wantin' him at Court. But please continue, I be sure they'll wait." He waved his hands at us to finish before darting back into the kitchen, and I assumed through the back door. What was that all about?

CHAPTER

8

OLD FRIENDS

I HAD TO admit I was sad when our make-out session turned dry humping got interrupted, and Chess left for his mysterious meeting in court. He didn't say which court, but I had a sneaky suspicion it was my mother calling him once again.

So, while Chess was away and Mop and Trip were doing God knew what, I decided to work on my glamour by myself. I just hoped Dorian kept busy doing whatever he was doing and left me alone. I hadn't seen hide or feather of him since the confrontation with Chess. Not that I was complaining, but losing my constant shadow was worrying, especially with the Shadow man on the loose.

The only mirror I didn't have covered was the one in the bathroom. I figured if Chess couldn't use it as a portal, then the Shadows wouldn't be able to either, or anyone else who decided to pay me a visit. Now that I knew there were others who were like me—well, not like me like me, but of more than one realm—I had to be careful whom I let into my sanctuary. I already had a parade of Fae coming in and out of my house on a whim.

My wet hair hung over my shoulders as I glared in the mirror. The stubborn blue color stared back at me. I had been trying for over an hour to get my eyes to change back to my original Christmas tree green, but the most I had been able to do was give myself a headache.

Before he left, Chess had suggested I find a picture of myself to use as a focal point, but after a quick search of my house and cell phone, I realized I didn't have any pictures of me to use. Apparently, I was really good about not getting my picture taken.

"Argh!" I stomped my foot when I opened my eyes to see blue ones staring back at me again. "I give up."

I tightened the towel around my top half and marched out of the bathroom into the hallway. I smacked into a solid warm body. My feet slipped. I landed hard my butt and my towel fell open, showing all my goods to the room.

"Well, hello, princess," said a voice I knew all too well from growing up in the Seelie Court.

I snatched my towel up from the ground and covered the ladies while glaring at the blonde intruder. "What the fuck, Jewels?"

I'd last seen Jewels at my own mourning party. Now, here he stood in my grandmother's hallway, thankfully more clothed than the last time. He was still shirtless, the barbells in his nipples glinted in the hall light, but the pants and boots were a far cry from the Speedo he wore the last time I saw him.

"Jewels? What are you doing?" Another familiar voice called out behind him. "Did you find her?"

"I found her all right." He leered at me, and I tightened my grip on the towel from my place on the floor.

"What do you mean?" Gab, the female equivalent of Jewels, appeared in the hallway. She glanced at her brother and when she saw me on the floor, shoved him out of the way. "Geez. What the hell is your problem? Here."

She held her hand out to me. A part of me was thrilled to see her. The part that remembered all the good times we had as best friends in my former life. She had been there for me when I came into my powers the first time. She had also been the one who pushed me to give my new fiancé a chance. Not that my Fae-self had any qualms about getting with the broody prince who ended up being one hell of a kisser. And it was her I should have run to when I caught said Prince in the arms of the fake me.

Her outstretched hand said more than words could ever. Funny, considering Gab's was the one person in the whole Underground who didn't know the word quiet. I hesitated, wondering which version of Gab was offering me help.

"Come on, I swear no funny business." She gave me a small, hesitant smile as if she was just as unsure as I was by her presence.

I slid my hand into hers and let her pull me to my feet. Keeping a firm grip on my towel, I swept into my room and slammed the door without a word. I dug through my pile of clothes on the ground, grabbing the first shirt and shorts I could find. While I was in the process of putting them on, a not so subtle argument broke out between the twins.

"Look what you did," Gab hissed from the other side of the door.

"I didn't do anything. She ran into me."

"Well, you shouldn't have been ogling at her. She's human now. They're more self-conscious than we are."

A smack sounded which was surely Gab whacking her brother over the head like she used to.

And like when we were younger, he only chuckled in response. "I don't know why. Even as a human, I would still like to lick every inch of her."

"Jewels. That's disgusting."

"Guys," I called out, opening the door, "I can hear you."

Gab rushed forward, shoving her brother out of the way. "Oh, Lynne. I mean Lady. I'm so sorry about Jewels. He's such an idiot. You know how he is always thinking with his little head. You do remember, don't you? I don't really know how this all works with you being you but not you, you know?"

I chuckled at the confusion on her face and led them to the living room. "Yes, I remember."

"Everything?" Jewels raised his eyebrow, a hopeful gleam in his eyes.

I knew what he hoped I would forget. There was a time, before I became engaged

110

to Dorian that I thought I might end up with Jewels. His name wasn't Jewels then. Though, in my opinion, Jewels was a far better name than Bastian. Sounded too close to bastard, though that was exactly what he was. A bastard.

One date and all dreams of joining the twin's family were destroyed. Jewels was one Fae who had no problem trying to take what didn't belong to him. And, like his sister, he had a problem with the definition of silence; the word *no* did not exist in his thick head.

"What do you think?" I asked him before turning to my maybe-sort-of best friend. "You know, it has been a while since I have been a part of the Seelie Court, but in the human world, it is customary to knock before entering someone's home."

Gab's, or Erydesa as she was once called, frowned and fidgeted in place, not like the confident Fae I knew at all.

I wasn't exactly what you would call a people person before. I was the one who would rather be in the library or walking the gardens than chatting up the visiting nobles. But Gab's was different. She lived to be in the spotlight and always tried to drag me into some gathering or another.

It was safe to say my Fae mother didn't exactly approve of Gab's. She wanted me to be out of sight and out of mind, while Gab's was all for showing the world what she had. I had gotten into more than my fair share of trouble because of her, but I wouldn't have had it any other way.

It was hard to believe the same Fae who snuck me out of my room at midnight to go skinny-dipping in the lake just over the palace walls was the same one standing in front of me. The uncertainty in her eyes as she exchanged a look with her brother wasn't someone I was used to seeing.

"We did knock. You didn't answer, and the door was open so we just—"

"Barged in unannounced?" I supplied. I sat on the couch while I let her stew in her own insecurity for a little longer. She was a total bitch to me at the party, so it was only fair to let her feel uncomfortable for a bit.

"No, I mean, yes," she fumbled over her words. Her face colored in a way I had always been jealous of.

After letting an awkward silence fill the room, I let a playful grin creep onto my face and a giggle escape my throat. Soon it turned into a full on laugh, and Gab's joined in after a moment.

"I told you there was nothing to worry about, sis. You two will always be inseparable." Jewels shook his head, his blonde hair whipping around him, but the bitterness in his voice not lost on me.

"Sorry, I couldn't help myself." I held my hand out to Gab's offering her to come sit by me on the couch. Jewels tried to occupy the other half, but I shot a glare at Jewels, and he changed his course to sit in one of the chairs instead.

Gab's sat next to me with a smile, but she shifted in her seat uncomfortably. She didn't seem to know how to act around me.

Sure, I was her long lost best friend from a lifetime ago, but I wasn't the same person before, as I'd made apparent to anyone who would listen. It would be as hard as trying to pick up where Dorian and I had left off, if not harder. Lovers came and went, and there was always that underlying wonder if you would mess up, but friends were forever—especially best friends.

I had never had to pretend with Gab's. She had always accepted me the way I was without trying to change me. Though, we would occasionally fight as friends did, we never let it ruin our friendship, just like I never tried to force her to give up her self-centered ways. That was just Gab's and it

113

would always be her. With friends like that, you either had to learn to deal with it or move on. I'd learned to deal with it when we were still in diapers. Not that we had diapers back then, but the premise was the same.

I grabbed her hand and pulled it into my lap as I snuggled into her side. While I tried to ignore most of the old part of me, having a friend by my side made me feel better. Safe. Like the world wasn't going to shit and my life wasn't a total mess. I could have sat there and basked in our friendship forever, but after a moment or two of silence, she finally spoke up.

"You're different. But oddly the same," she mused.

"Well, that is bound to happen when one's soul is reincarnated as a different species." I shrugged my shoulders.

"So, what happened to you?" Jewels leaned forward in his chair, the worry on his face gone now.

I frowned at him in thought. How did I explain what occurred to me when I wasn't even sure I knew what transpired? The one person who could answer all my questions had been conveniently silent when I had actually been at its feet. Or roots, for that matter.

That annoying tree had no problem pestering me to come home and hijacking my visions with cryptic messages, but when I was actually in front of it—where it wanted me to be—it was silent. I didn't know if it was because of how wilted and pathetic it had looked, or if it was just being a pain in the ass, but I'd had enough secrets to last me a lifetime.

Gab's squeezed my hand. "How about an easier question?"

I blew out a relieved breath. "Yes, please."

Before Gab's could ask her question, Jewels jumped in again, "What about his highness? What are you going to do about him? Are you going to marry him?"

"Not that it is any of your business, but that is not any easier to answer than how this all happened." I glared at Jewels, who slumped back in his seat with a pout on his face.

"How about we start with what do we call you?" Gab's offered with a small smile. "Do you want to go by Lady? Or your human name? What was it again?"

"Kat. And either one is fine, really. Just don't call me Lynne." I snapped my gaze to Jewels, the warning clear in my eyes. "I have a hard enough time keeping things straight up here, and it will be an easy reminder that I might be me, but I'm not me." I ended with a lame chuckle.

"I like it. Makes you more like one of us already. Lady it is." Gab's pulled her legs under her and turned on the couch to look at me.

"What?" I asked after she continued to stare at me without speaking.

"You know, you could glamour yourself back to your human look, right?" She cocked her head, picking at the strands of my blonde hair.

"I'm working on it, but it's hard to do in this body." I gave an aggravated sigh. "Nothing seems to work the same way it did when I was in my Fae body. Everything is harder. I couldn't even glamour my eyes to my normal color. I had to be looking at Chess to even get anything to happen at all."

"The half-breed was helping you?" Jewels laughed and, much to my dismay, his sister joined in.

"What's wrong with that?" I looked between them. "He's the only one that was around to help, and I certainly wasn't going to ask you-know-who to teach me."

I didn't know why, but my comment only made them laugh harder.

116

"I'm sorry." Gab's giggled. "We aren't laughing at you."

"Speak for yourself," Jewels popped in.

Gab's glared at her brother, the blue of her eyes becoming glacial, before turning back to me with an amused smile. "Like I said, we aren't laughing at you. We are laughing at the thought that the half-breed—"

This time, I interrupted her. "Chess."

"Right, Chess." She gave me a curious look but continued on, "It's the thought that he could in any way know what it is like to be a full-blooded Fae."

"But I'm not a full-blooded Fae," I interjected. "I technically have human blood with a Fae soul. Nothing to do with my blood at all, really."

"But you are showing signs of your original full Fae powers, aren't you?"

"Yes, and more are showing up every day. I could probably make things grow on their own if I could figure out how to get my magic to cooperate." I turned my gaze to the back of the house where the garden was.

It would be so much easier to grow my own vegetables if I had a little magic in my arsenal. Not like being able to grow the world's largest tomato was high on my priority list.

"Well, you can't very well expect a half-breed to be able to instruct you. It would be like asking a blind man to tell you what color the sky is. He might know what color it is supposed to be, but that doesn't mean he knows what color it is."

I was trying hard not to lash out at Gab's, but every time she said the word *half-breed* my eye twitched. I didn't know if it was because they were talking about Chess, or because I, myself, could be described as a half-breed. All I did know was that the condescending tone pissed me off more than I could imagine.

"Fine," I snapped out, cutting Gab's off mid-rant. "Why don't you tell me how it's done, then?"

She pursed her lips in that bitchy way I had only seen aimed at me when we first met in my human form and the few times I snapped at her about her holier-than-thou attitude.

"Look. I'm just trying to help, but if you don't want it..." She stood from the couch and gestured for Jewels to follow. "We can just go."

I didn't move from my seat. She was trying to power play me. I knew she was, and usually, I would just apologize and plead for her to stay, but not this time. I wasn't a pushover anymore that didn't like to make waves. Someone who just let the road of life direct her wherever it may. I was the fucking driver this time.

"Maybe you should," I said evenly.

She paused, her brow crinkled. Her blue eyes locked with her brother, who only shrugged and headed toward the back door. With the bastard out of the way, she turned back to me, her gaze softened.

"Look, Lady." She brushed her hand through her long hair, the way she did when she was trying to seem confident, but didn't realize it was her nervous tell. "I know you have a soft spot for the half—I mean Chess—but you can't expect to learn what you need to know from him. Or expect to get the whole truth about what really happened while you were gone."

"What really happened?" I asked, ignoring the whole point of our conversation.

"That's a story for another day. It's too long to get into, and I have a date to get ready for." She smoothed her hands down her body. Her pants and trendy top morphed into a form-fitting, ice blue dress that glittered in the light. "How do I look?"

"How did you do that?" I gaped.

She made an impatient sound. "That's what I'm trying to tell you." She reached over and pulled me out of my seat. "You are making it too hard. You don't need to focus, and you don't need to build your magic up. You don't remember having to do any of that stuff before, do you?"

I shook my head.

"Exactly. You don't have to think about it, just make it happen." She pumped my hands with each word, exciting and unhelpful at the same time.

"Okay."

Dropping my hands, she primped her hair with her hand. "Well, I have to get going. I'll stop by again, and we can catch up some more."

"But what about teaching me to glamour?"

She waved at me. "You'll be fine. Just remember. Don't think, just make it happen." Her hair whipped around her as she sauntered toward the back door. Then she paused. "And don't trust that cat. He might be a pretty face, but you should know better than anyone else that isn't always a good thing."

As she disappeared through the kitchen door, I plopped back down on the couch, lost in my own thoughts. Unfortunately, I did know what she meant, but I doubted she knew anything about the Shadow man, or what lay behind his own pretty face. Her warning about Chess had to be her biased towards half-breeds. There was no way that anything as bad as the Shadow man was hiding behind Chess' delicious physique. Or, at least, I hoped not.

CHAPTER

9

PRACTICE

STARING AT MYSELF in the bathroom mirror again, I tried to pump myself up to finally glamour my eyes.

Just do it. Don't think about it. Just do it. I took a few breaths in and then out. Here we go.

I slowly blinked as I thought of what my eyes used to look like. As I opened my eyes, the ice blue of my pupils melted into forest green.

I did it! I couldn't believe I actually did it. I thought Gab's was full of shit when she told me it was just that easy, but the little snot had been right. I had started to believe it was just me, that I was defective in some way and could only use my powers when I was having some kind of emotional breakdown. Though, I knew it wasn't true, because I used it back with the glowing fruit.

Not wanting to dwell on my own misgivings, or get into the never-ending spiral that was the mystery of the talking tree, I tried to focus on the good.

I shook my head with a silly smile. "It was so easy."

"What was that easy?" a voice purred from behind me.

I glanced in the mirror at Chess' leaning form in the bathroom door, and an accomplished smile spread across my face.

"Is anything different?" Whipping around, I fluttered my eyelashes at him.

"Well, I don't know." He uncrossed his arms and sauntered over to me. He was unglamoured again, and his tail swung behind him, adding a bit more swagger to his step. His vest parted with each step, giving me small glimpses of his chest.

He brushed a strand of hair behind my ear. "Nope, still as beautiful as ever."

With his eyes intently focused on mine, my lids fluttered down and then up as my face filled with heat. It was weird how the words were not perverted, or flirty in any way, but still caused my heart to thud hard in my chest. I didn't know how to act around this version of Chess. With most

123

guys, I'd laugh and push them away in an attempt to hide my reaction, but with him, all I could manage was a giggle.

"My eyes, silly." I bit my lip and glanced back up to meet his gaze, but inwardly smacked myself for sounding like such a ditz. I wasn't one of those girls that used the word *silly*. I hated those girls.

"Oh, those." Chess trailed his clawed finger along the arch of my cheek. "I see you've been practicing."

"A little bit." I cleared my throat, side stepping him and exiting the bathroom, hoping he didn't catch my half-truth. I seemed to always be getting caught in my towel, and a small cloth was not a good idea around the frisky feline.

"What are you doing here, anyway?" I asked over my shoulder as I delved through my clothes.

"It's Sunday, remember?"

It was Sunday, and that meant dinner with the family. Back in New York, I would be curled up on the couch with some Chinese food and binge watching the latest paranormal series that included ripped guys who didn't wear their shirt most of the time. In Iowa, though, Sunday dinner was an affair that yoga pants and Thursday's T-shirt would get me a lecture about until I gave into my mother's urging to wear one of her dresses.

Changing directions, I pulled open the closet door and rummaged through the clothes that had fallen to the bottom. I grabbed the least wrinkled dress and turned back to Chess.

"You aren't being honest, Kat," he said, sounding hurt.

I frowned, my stomach tightened in knots. I didn't think repeating what happened with my old friends would be a good idea, not only because I didn't want to injure Chess' feelings, but because I didn't want to have the conversation about what my relationship with them before was like. So I did what Fae did best: be evasive as fuck.

"I just did it." I threw the dress on the bed, a dark blue t-shirt style that would hit me just below mid-thigh. It happened to be the only dress my mother wouldn't give me crap about and still wasn't too girly for my tastes.

"I see." Chess spread himself out on my bed, looking very much at home, and too perfect in my room. He fingered the dress while he watched me carefully.

Avoiding his gaze, I went in search of a pair of acceptable shoes. In most cases, I would have gone straight for the flats. For some reason, my hands landed on the only pair of heels I owned instead.

They weren't expensive by any means. They were black with a low, two-inch heel and a strap that wrapped around my ankle. They weren't 'fuck me heels' by society standards, but I'd never had any complaints.

"I suppose the scent of a certain pair of twins I caught on my way in had nothing to do with it?" his voice was dark and sensual but had a bite to it that made me wince.

"You can't wear that." I attempted to evade his question as I slipped the dress over my head and the towel.

Though, the mirror was still covered by a sheet, I could see a faint outline of Chess as he moved from the bed. I let the towel pool at my feet as a pair of strong, warm arms wrapped around me.

"You don't need to hide from me, Kat," he murmured in my hair. "I know what those in both courts say about my kind. I've had time to get used to it. So, do not worry about sparing my feelings."

"Doesn't mean it is right," I countered, acutely aware of how naked I was underneath the dress.

"Right or wrong. What does it matter? It is what it is, and there is no use in worrying your pretty little head about it now." He gave me a squeeze and released me without more than a slight caress.

The air rippled around me as it did when magic was afoot, and I stepped out of the towel at my feet to see what had happened.

"How do I look?" he asked.

With his glamour back in place, Chess no longer had his adorable ears. His pink hair was braided and blond and it lay across his shoulder. His bare chest was covered with a dark plum colored button-up and was tucked into a pair of black dress pants with matching dress shoes. He looked normal, and yet still, otherworldly.

"Well?" He inclined his head to the side, a small grin on his face displaying the lack of fangs in his mouth.

"You look like you stepped out of one of those fashion magazines." Just then, my gaze caught sight of said magazine sitting on the floor by the bed. It was opened up to a page showing a male model with the exact same outfit, though Chess wore it infinitely better. "You did jack that from a magazine! Isn't that cheating?"

He gave an elegant shrug. "I only used what was at my disposal. Do you not like it?"

He grabbed my hand, pulling me to him as I tried to turn for the door. Instead of touching the cloth of his new shirt, I felt the warm skin of his chest. To make matters worse on my rising pulse, his invisible tail whipped out and slid up the length of my legs beneath my dress. It wasn't like I wasn't used to him groping me, but not seeing it when I could feel it made it so much creepier, and yet weirdly exciting. It was going to be one of those kinds of nights, I could already tell.

When his tail got too close to my bare butt, I pulled myself away from his grasp without answering his question. Grabbing a pair of underwear from the laundry pile, I inelegantly pulled them on while he watched with laughter in his eyes. Ignoring him, I shoved my feet into my shoes and kneeled down to buckle the straps. When those were done, I grabbed my keys off the nightstand and headed out the door with Chess in tow.

I stepped out onto the front porch, and he made a noise behind me.

"Where are we going?"

I rolled my eyes at him. "To my mom's, of course."

"But how will we be getting there?"

"In my car, of course." I headed to my car.

It wasn't an expensive car: a small, four-door blue sedan that I had driven since high school. It was old, and the stereo system was out of date and crackled sometimes. But it was mine, and mine alone. I had bought it with my own money from my part-time job at Dairy Queen. Not that I had to work—my parents would have been more than happy to buy me a car—but it would have been some extravagant foreign car that cost more than what was normal for a sixteen-year-old's first car should.

Chess snorted behind me, and my hand paused on the door handle.

"What?"

"Why use that when we could use a mirror and be there in no time?" His voice was arrogant but had an underlying nervousness to it.

"Are you scared, Chess?" A small, teasing smile crept up onto my face.

"No," he snapped. "I just do not see the point of riding in that." He pointed his finger at my car, and I bristled. "We could just as well use magic."

129

"And where, pray tell, would we come out at?" I crossed my arms; annoyed he was dissing my car. "We don't have mirrors linked up to everyone's houses here, and even if we did, I could imagine all kinds of trouble coming from people entering without permission. Not to forget, these are humans, it would be weird for us just to pop up in their house unannounced. Besides, I don't think this is about using magic at all. I think you're scared." A delighted glee filled my face. I danced a little jiggle, wiggling my hips back and forth, calling out in a singsong voice, "Chess is a big, old, scaredy cat."

"Fine. Let's get in your death trap." He marched past me and shoved himself into my car, slamming the door behind him.

Frowning, I opened the driver side of the car and slid in. Had I taken it too far? I put the key in the ignition and started the engine, glancing at Chess, who was digging his nails into the seat of the car.

"Hey." I grabbed his hand and gave it a reassuring squeeze. "Relax. You have nothing to worry about. I'm a great driver."

Dropping his hand, I threw the car into reverse and peeled out of the driveway. Chess yowled in protest, and I tried to repress a chuckle. This was definitely going to be an interesting dinner.

"THAT WASN'T SO bad, was it?" I asked when we arrived at my parent's house.

Chess didn't answer, and I turned to look at him. I tried not to laugh. His hair stood on end and his glamour flickered in place, making his already petrified eyes even more so by the changing of his pupil back and forth from human to feline.

"Chess?" I spoke in a soft voice so as not to spook him. I held my hand out. He turned to look at me, but it was like he didn't really see me. He blinked over and over, and then he was out the car door, and making his way up to my family's house.

Jumping out of the car, I hurried after him as fast as my heels would let me. I caught up with him as I made my way up the walkway of the old Victorian style house my mother was so proud of. Keeping history alive, she liked to say. But to me, it was gaudy and screamed, 'Look how much money we have!' It was three stories, with way more rooms than anyone needed, let alone an old married couple whose kids were out of the house.

"Chess, are you all right?"

"I'm fine," he muttered as we headed up the steps.

I didn't need Fae senses to tell it was a lie. His shoulders were stiff, and his hands were clenched into fists. I was about to call him out on his bluff when the front door opened to reveal my mother's housekeeper, Hillary.

Hillary was an older woman whose pale skin was only made paler by her pitch-black hair that had started going white while I was away at college. She had sharp eyes, a grim smile, and eyes that saw everything a little kid did, even when in a different part of the monstrous house.

My sister and I despaired whenever Hillary was tasked with watching us for the day. It meant no playing around, and we'd end up doing more chores than usual. One time, I was in the kitchen trying to sneak a snack when Hillary's grim voice called out from the third floor.

"Katherine, get out of the kitchen and come help me clean up your disaster of a room."

I didn't know how she knew I was in the kitchen, but she always did. I swore it was witchcraft of some kind. Linda and I always got in trouble for doing something we normally wouldn't have gotten caught with our mother watching us.

Those same sharp eyes penetrated through me now as if she could tell there was more different about me than my hair color.

"Katherine," she greeted with as much warmth as she could muster.

"Hillary," I returned with a nod.

"And this is?" She tilted her chin toward Chess.

"Oh." I placed my hand on his arm. The bare muscle flexed beneath my fingers, reminding me of what hid behind his glamour. "This is my friend, Chess. Mom invited him to dinner."

Sunday dinner was usually a family affair and only serious boyfriends, or the occasional benefactor my father needed to impress was allowed to join.

Her hawk eyes narrowed in on Chess. He didn't make any move to defend himself or greet her, so unlike his usual flirty self. It made me worry the car ride had affected him more than I thought.

We waited while Hillary came to her own conclusions, none of which she shared with us. She sniffed and opened the door wider, allowing us into the foyer.

Shutting the door behind us, she gestured toward the door to the right. "Your mother is in the sitting room, and I wouldn't keep her waiting."

The last part was more a warning than anything, letting me know my mother was in one of her moods again. I repressed a sigh and hoped she would calm down when she remembered Chess was here.

"Hillary!" My mother's voice screeched through the house. "Who is at the door? Is that Katherine I hear?"

"Yes, Mom. No need to shout." I stepped into the sitting room, my shoulders back and ready for a stiff one. Drink, that was.

"There you are." My mother stood from her seat on the couch next to my sister, Miss Fucking Perfect, and her fiancé, Mister Fucking Perfect. "We were beginning to think you weren't going to show up again."

And the first round had begun.

"I couldn't very well not show up after you asked so nicely." I smiled sweetly, approaching my chuckling father who sat in his favorite chair by the mantel. "Hi, Daddy."

I bent down and kissed his cheek.

"Hello, sweetheart." He wrapped an arm around me in a warm hug.

My father was almost ten years older than my mother and had already begun to bald so much that he had shaved it all off, leaving only his red goatee that was the same shade as my hair. His eyes were the deep forest green that matched mine, except for the age lines that surrounded his. He always had a smile for me and had never once raised a hand or voice at my mother.

He had been my rock in every difficult bump in my life. When I broke up with my first and only boyfriend in high school, he was there to wipe my tears. When Mom was being unbearable, he was there to calm me down from doing something rash. As an actuary, he had more patience than a saint, and I never did find out if being married to my mother was a self-inflicted punishment or not. Though, he swore Mom was more like me when she was younger, I didn't believe it.

A throat cleared next to me, reminding me of my guest's presence.

"Katherine, you are being very rude." My mother latched onto Chess' arm, pulling him toward a chair.

If she noticed she was touching skin instead of the cloth of his shirt, she didn't give it away. Chess let himself be seated, and she perched on the arm of the chair. I sat on the arm of my father's chair and watched my family interact with Chess.

Seeming to notice Chess' distress, my mother did what she did best—poked at it. "Are you all right, dear? You don't seem to be yourself?"

Chess glanced up at my mother and offered a weak smile before taking her hand in his, giving it a brush of his lips. "How could I not be with such company surrounding me?"

Linda giggled on the couch. "Where did you find him? He sounds like a fairy prince from one of your books."

If I was the spitting image of my dad, then Linda was everything that embodied my mother. Blonde hair cropped in a fashionable angled bob and subtle makeup, combined with a smart, pale pink blouse with a matching skirt. Kitten heels completed her ensemble and, to make the image even more picturesque, her new fiancé, Simon, sat quietly next to her with a polite smile on his face.

I'd only met Simon once before, and he had as much character as a lima bean.

My eyes landed on Chess, and I smirked. "Oh, you know, just something I ordered out of a magazine."

Chess cracked the first real smile since we had gotten in my car.

"So, how did you two get here? Not in that monstrosity you call a car, I hope." My mom asked.

"Hey!" I stood from my seat. "There is nothing wrong with my car. It runs fine."

She ignored me and gave Chess a pitying look. "I hope you at least didn't let her drive. Katherine has many hidden skills, but driving is not one of them."

I ground my teeth at her blatant jab. I watched Chess' face for a reaction to her words, pleading in my eyes. I didn't know how much more of my mother's quips I could take before I blew up the house.

Playing the part of perfect dinner guest, Chess smiled. "I don't know about that. Kat was a wonderful driver. I felt like I could have slept for days knowing I was in her capable hands."

"Yeah in a coma," my sister muttered.

"Linda, I think we've had enough of that," my father, God bless him, said in an easy tone. "Isn't dinner supposed to be ready soon?"

He glanced down at his watch, an old birthday gift I had given to him. It was a Walmart knockoff. My mother had scoffed, but he still wore it every day.

As if knowing he was asking, Hillary stepped into the doorway. "Dinner is served."

"Wonderful." My mother moved from her spot and gestured to the door. "Shall we all adjourn to the dining room?"

As we made our way out of the living room, I grabbed Chess' hand in mine, pulling him behind everyone.

"Thank you," I whispered keeping my eyes downcast.

He squeezed back with one hand and tilted my chin up with the other. "Think nothing of it."

The softness in his eyes made my breath catch. He could be so sweet when he wanted to be. Then his tail took that moment to grope my ass. I squeaked in surprise. Knocking his invisible tail away, I gave him a chastising glare, though my heart wasn't in it.

As we settled in our seats at the table, Simon cleared his throat.

"So, Chess. That is an unusual name. What exactly is it that you do?"

"Do?" Chess tilted his head to the side in a very cat-like manner.

I hid my smile behind my napkin.

"Excuse Simon." My sister placed her hand on her fiancé's arm. "He means, what is your occupation, your job? You must be some kind of actor or model, right?"

I didn't like the way my sister was assessing Chess. She had that slight hungry look in her eyes that most women got when dealing with him.

"What do I do?" Chess repeated the question back slowly, before giving me a questioning side glance.

I nodded, giving him permission to say whatever he wanted. I was curious to see how he would handle their questions as well. Would he mention the Fae world?

He sat up higher in his seat, giving off a commanding presence that had the rest of the room's occupants leaning in to listen.

"I'm the moderator," he said, matter-of-fact. Most people would have been like 'I'm a doctor' or 'I'm a model,' but Chess in the Fae realm was The Moderator. The one who

140

settled all disputes between the Fae kingdoms.

When I was the princess, we didn't have a moderator. With the UnSeelie Court at fault for my suicide, everything had pretty much defaulted to my mother's decisions, though, sometimes there would be a dispute between the two realms that had to be handled by a third party and that's where Chess came in.

"He's the moderator between two companies and sometimes he handles civil disputes. Isn't that right?" I lifted my brow at him, expecting him to play along.

"Right," he drew out.

"So, how much money does that kind of position pay?" Simon asked.

I almost fell out of my seat.

Maybe I had misjudged this guy. He at least seemed to have some kind of brain in his head and no filter to his mouth. I suddenly couldn't wait until their wedding.

"Simon!" my sister gasped. "You shouldn't ask such things."

While she chastised her fiancé, I could still see that she wanted to know as well.

I reached for the glass to occupy my mouth while I thought of an answer, but Chess beat me to it.

"Oh, quite well. I am provided with an unlimited supply of willing companions to meet my every need."

I sighed at his response and took a deep drink from my glass. At least one of us knew what was going on.

"And you know the occasional virgin to keep things interesting."

I started coughing, choking on my tea as it went down the wrong pipe. The cup spilled onto the table and into my lap. A warm hand patted me on the back, but I waved it away, and I drew in a breath.

"Are you all right, dear?" My mother's concerned voice pulled my attention. "Hillary! Get Katherine a towel for her dress." She turned her attention back to me. "You'll want to get that dry cleaned. No need to ruin your only suitable outfit."

I refrained from rolling my eyes since my throat was still burning, and I turned to Hillary as she held out a towel for me to dry off with.

"It is upsetting, really," my mother continued, speaking directly to Chess. "She has such a nice figure, but she hides it behind all those frumpy clothes. It's no wonder she never finds a date."

"I attract guys just fine, Mom," I growled, patting my lap with the towel harder than I needed to.

"No suitable ones in any case." She turned her gaze to Chess as if realizing her mistake. "Of course not you, dear. Katherine certainly lucked out with you. But you should have seen some of the boys she would bring home with her. Remember, Linda?"

My sister gave me an apologetic look and muttered, "I remember."

My eyes bore holes into my lap as my mother listed out all the boys I had ever brought home. Which wasn't all that many. I learned quickly not to bring anyone I actually liked to the house, or they'd run for the hills before dinner was ever served. Except for one time.

"And what about that one boy? The one from the south side who lived by the railroad tracks? What was his name?" she mused aloud.

"Eric," I reluctantly supplied, knowing, and yet dreading, what she was going to say.

"Yes, that was it." She waved her finger at me. "He was such an attractive boy and had such great manners. It was too bad his family was such heathens. He would have

143

been a great catch otherwise. I hear he went on to work at the mill just like his father. Sad, really."

Anger pulsated through me, and my magic coursed through my veins. With my mother, my anger always just simmered below the surface. I was surprised it had waited that long to make its presence known. Now that it had, I knew I had to get out of there before I destroyed something important. Like my mother's face.

I shoved back my chair, startling the whole table. Keeping my eyes down, I muttered an apology to my father as I hurried from the dining room. My mother's voice called after me, but all I could think about was getting out before my skin exploded.

CHAPTER

FAMILIES ARE THE WORST

I RUSHED FROM the house, the front door slamming behind me. As I stepped off the porch, my heel snapped under me, throwing me toward the ground. I turned sideways to fall on the grass instead of the hard concrete.

The instant my hands touched the ground, my magic seeped out of me and into the lawn. I could physically see the pulse of my magic as it flowed from my hands and into the foliage around me. It was like little tiny green veins of energy were fleeing from me and going into the earth. I watched in amazement as the grass grew several inches longer and tiny flowers sprouted up from the yard.

The only thing that came to my mind was my mother was going to be pissed. She loved a well kept yard. She loved a well kept everything. When she saw that her immaculate yard was now a gardener's nightmare, she was not going to be happy.

A small giggle came out of me. Then that giggle transformed into a full on laugh. A laugh that even to my ears was beginning to sound hysterical.

"Kat," Chess' voice was quiet behind me, but I paid him no attention, my mind high on the magic pulsing out of me. I would have thought using my magic would have tired me out, but all I felt was powerful. Indestructible. Something I had never felt before, but wanted nothing more than to feel again.

"Katherine." His voice was closer now and more forceful.

Again, I didn't answer. I watched the ground beneath me as it grew and changed. What would happen if I forced more of myself into it? With that thought, the green veins turned into thick ropes of power. It surged from me and forced a multitude of flowers and mushrooms not of this world to sprout from their earthly prison.

Even with the new force of power, it wasn't enough. I needed more. I needed to feel the very core of the earth beneath my feet. I needed—

146

"Lynne!" Chess' use of my Fae name cut through my power hungry haze.

I pulled my hands away from the ground and watched as the newly grown plant life began to wither and die before my eyes. A small part of me wept for the loss, but the other part was in horror of what had happened. I had never been so consumed by my magic as a human or a Fae. As a Fae, I had been limited by the rules of our world. Not as many rules as there were now, but rules that tired one out after a few minutes of full powered magic. The power I had just shown would never have happened in the Fae Realm. At least, not to a full-blooded Fae.

"Come, we should leave before someone sees you." Chess ushered me toward the car.

Inside, I turned the engine and eased out of the driveway. I only remembered pulling onto the road before we were once again back in front of my grandmother's small farm house. Just the sight of it caused exhaustion to press down on me.

The driver's side door opened, and Chess appeared before me. I gazed up at him with weak eyes. The sudden use of all that power had been exhilarating at first, but now I just felt drained. The very act of breathing became a chore itself.

Without asking, Chess slipped his arm under my legs and pulled me into his embrace. My arms automatically wrapped around his neck, and I buried my face in his collar, the smell of him filling my senses. I let him carry me to the house, and then into my bedroom, where he sat me down on the bed as if I was the most fragile thing in the world. Kneeling at my feet, he unhooked my shoes and slipped them off, and then eased my legs onto the bed.

Usually, I was happy with quiet. Too much chatter gave me a headache, but right now, the quiet, more specifically, the quiet coming from the only male in the room, was killing me.

"I'm sorry about that. My mother..." I started, not quite up to defending her. "She's kind of a bitch, but she does have her moments. Sometimes."

I gave a weary shrug that even to me was not comforting.

Chess sat next to me on the bed, silently watching my face. I could see the wheels turning behind his sparkling green eyes. When he finally spoke, the words that came out of his mouth were not what I expected.

"You should go back."

148

"Back? Back where? To my mom's?" I scoffed, snuggling down under the covers. "I don't think so."

"No." His voice was small but forceful. "Back to the Underground."

I sat up from the comfortable blanket cocoon and glared at him.

He pressed his hand against my mouth. "Now before you get upset. Listen for a moment, Kat."

Frowning at his hand, and half tempted to lick it, I nodded.

"Half-breeds," he started, "we're different—from other Fae. As you've noticed, we don't have to obey the same sort of rules that are in place for the rest of our kind. Now, in certain circumstances, this wouldn't matter since most of us don't have much power to begin with."

I opened my mouth to argue against him degrading his own power, but he cut me off.

"Not all of us, but some of us. Those of us that don't have much power, well, we don't live long. As you know, the Underground is not a forgiving place, and it seeks to destroy or conquer anything different from it. Now this might not be winning me points on my argument for you to return, but there are benefits to being back in our world."

He reached his hand up and cupped my face. I watched his eyes for some sort of clue to what he was thinking but didn't get much. I wished he had dropped his glamour so I could watch the telltale sign of his emotions in his tail and ears.

"What happened today, just now, isn't something that should have happened." He lowered his hand from my cheek and stared off into space. "You are more powerful now as a human than you could have ever been as a Fae, and because of that, the limitations you had before won't be there to stop you."

This time, I had to speak up, "Why should I need them? I don't need anyone to tell me when I've had enough."

"Is that how you felt today?" His eyes had a knowing look in them. "Did you feel like you needed to stop?"

"No." I thought back to how I felt. "I needed more. Like I could do anything. I wanted to do it. I didn't want to stop."

"And there lies the problem. We don't have the fail-safe the full-blooded Fae do. I don't know the mechanics behind it. Whether it's brain waves, or just a hiccup in the womb, but what matters is we're different. We don't know when we need to pull back from the edge before we start siphoning others, and then eventually, our own life force. And that is exactly why the Shadows want us so badly."

The new knowledge did not set well with me. I was a ticking time bomb ready to go off at the first angry fit. Not only that, but if the Shadow man somehow convinced me to join their little cause, they would also have unlimited power to bend to their will. That was something I wasn't going to let happen.

"Your mother loves you."

I snorted at his change in topic.

He narrowed his eyes. "She might not be able to show it in the way you want her to, but she does. You are lucky to have a family, any family that would pay you any sort of attention. Whether you want it or not. You happen to have two families. Two families that want you with them, even if it means being something you are not. I know I was the one who urged you to be a dandelion, but maybe being a rose is what you need right now. And what might be safer for everyone involved."

"Is that what you did?" I argued. "Did what your family wanted you to do so you could fit in?"

A sad, bitter smile crossed his face. "I didn't have the luxury of that choice."

Remorse filled me for bringing it up, but I had to know. "Why?"

"Before you were a human, were there many half-breeds?"

I actually hadn't thought much about it. I knew there were more now than there had been when I was the princess. Sometimes a Fae could mate with a human, or on a rarer occasion, a Seelie with an UnSeelie. But since the amount of Fae children born had declined, I had assumed it was because of all the mixing of the bloods and thought nothing of it.

"Why are there more now than before? I thought Mother wanted to stop all that because it was causing the Fae to become barren."

Chess gave a disgusted laugh. "Not hardly. You, my dear princess, have it the wrong way around."

"What do you mean?"

"Crossbreeding with another Fae and the humans was not the problem. The problem was too much inbreeding of the Fae amongst themselves."

My brows furrowed together in confusion. "Then why wouldn't they encourage crossbreeding if we needed new blood?"

"Power," he stated. "Crossbreeding with the humans was lessening the magical pool of power in the Fae realm, and your mother couldn't have that. So she stopped it."

"Then why let them do it now? What changed?"

"Oh, she didn't let them do anything." He gave a dark chuckle. "After your unfortunate mishap, her plans to conquer the Shadows with the power of the combined realms were squashed. She needed someone that had unlimited power to use against the Shadows, and since she couldn't get it from you, her own child, she forced it from elsewhere."

A sick feeling filled me as the words sank in. My mother, the Seelie Queen, had orchestrated the creation of hundreds of half-blooded Fae children, all for the means to conquer the Shadows. While I understood the need to keep the realms safe, forcing the couplings was too much. But what didn't make sense was if she made her power source, why was the Shadow man still a threat?

"What failed? Why aren't the Shadows gone?" My eyes flickered toward my mirror as the words left my mouth. The very sound of their name made my skin crawl as if eyes were on me.

"Who knows?" He shrugged before he stood up from his place on the bed and moved to the door.

I could tell he was keeping something from me but didn't think pushing would be the right answer. He'd tell me when he was ready. He went for the door, and panic rose up in me. The new knowledge coupled with my mother's words had beaten me down and made me weak and frightened to be in my own head.

"Wait," I said.

He paused, looking back at me.

"I don't want to be alone right now."

He let his glamour melt off him as he made his way back to my side. I shifted over on the bed so he could lie down beside me. Lying next to him in the bed, I was stiff as a board. I had asked him to stay, but I didn't even know what that meant. Or what he thought it meant.

After a moment or two of awkward silence, he wrapped his arm around me and pulled me to his chest. His finger covered my mouth to any protest.

"Sleep, my dandelion. Just sleep."

I let the sound of his heart beating against my ear rock me to sleep, but my head was heavy and full of thoughts of magic and darkness to come.

CHAPTER

WHAT'S DONE IN THE DARK

THE SOUND OF my name being whispered in my ear tugged me from my sleep. A light wisp of a touch trailed down my arm, and I shivered. I fought to stay in the dream I was having about a certain cat, a tub of rocky road ice cream, and a deliciously cold wrestling match. The voice wasn't having any of it, though. I cracked my eyes open.

I glanced to my right to find Chess still in my bed, curled up in the fetal position, his tail flicking back and forth in his sleep. A small smile played on my face, and I almost lay back down next to him. Something in my peripherals moved. The mirror I kept covered in my bedroom was bare, the sheet nowhere in sight. Creepy smoke spilled off the surface.

The smoke rolled across my ankles when I lowered my feet to the floor. It was cool against my skin but didn't lash out, instead urging me forward toward the mirror.

The mirror reflected the bedroom with Chess' form in my bed, the room darkened by the night shadows. Then the mirror rippled and flowed, flickering between my room and the mushroom town, before finally settling on the orchard.

Stepping up to the mirror, I gazed into it, trying to depict what it was trying to show me. Was it the Shadows finally coming for me to claim their queen? Or something else altogether? I reached my hand up to touch the surface, and as if sensing my movement, the scene changed. Speeding up like a moving car, it zoomed through the trees, ignoring the door to the Between, and aiming for a hidden alcove that was covered by overgrown bushes.

All at once, I knew who was calling out to me. Even though the voice that had said my name wasn't the same voice I had heard before as it tried to coax me back to Iowa, it had the same sense of urgency to it. The same need for me to be there. One thing I had learned out of all my recent adventures was to listen to that voice. So, as the image came to a sudden stop in front of the all-knowing tree, I stepped through the mirror's surface.

My bare feet landed on the dirt ground before the tree. The stone walls that closed it off from the rest of the Underground stood tall and imposing. The area seemed darker, more foreboding than the last time I had been there. No doubt because of the wilted vision of the tree in front of me.

Before the tree hadn't seemed so decrepit, just barren of fruit or leaves. Now, it seemed to bend as if it was too much effort to stand tall. I felt a sudden urge to touch the trunk, as if I could somehow discern what had happened to it.

I moved toward the tree, but a voice resounded around me.

"You have come to us."

I halted, and then stepped back at the voice coming from the tree. Part of me was hoping to finally get some answers, while the other half was mostly wondering where the heck it was talking out of.

"Well, you didn't give me much of a choice." I crossed my arms over my chest. "Do you always hijack people's dreams to talk to them?"

The tree didn't answer for a moment, and then it finally spoke, sounding weaker than before, "We are not long for this world. Speaking through dreams is easier."

"You're dying? But what am I supposed to do? I don't even know how to defeat the Shadows yet." I was beginning to feel a bit screwed over. They were the ones who had brought me here in the first place. The ones who wanted me to 'save them.' Now they were going to go off and die on me without so much as a way to save them? Hell no.

"Our time is coming to an end. We are no longer needed. But your time is still to come. There will be much need for you from both Fae and human alike."

"Yeah, yeah. Everyone loves me. But what am I supposed to do about the Shadows?" Irritation scratched at me.

"All will come to pass in time. You will find your strength but a sacrifice must be made. Debts must be repaid."

"That is not helpful at all!" I cried out. I didn't care if they knew it would be all right. I needed to know what was going to happen. What sacrifice? What debts?

"We help when needed." The sound of their voice became more distant and hollow. I had to strain to hear them at all. I tried to step forward to demand them to tell me what was happening, but the moment my foot moved the scene changed.

I was no longer in the alcove where the tree was withering away but in the middle of a forest. I turned in a circle, frantic to find my way back to the tree. To demand it to give me some answers. With nothing but dark trees surrounding me, I had little choice but to pick a direction and start walking.

"You don't want to be going that way, Lady," a familiar voice said behind me.

I spun around to find the Shadow man lounging in Hatter's chair, where it and the table had not been before.

"You never know what kind of baddies could be lurking in the dark."

He had traded out his black suit for one of a more eye-catching blue, his feet were propped up on the edge of the table as he leaned back in Hatter's chair as if he owned it. The curve of the smile on his face caused my skin to crawl. He had that look that tiptoed the line of wanting to fuck me and devour me at the same time. For all I knew, he probably did.

"What am I doing here?" I edged around the other end of the table, where Door Mouse usually sat, to keep a safe distance between us.

"Why to have tea, of course?" He gestured to the table where it had been laid out with a tea set and cookies. My stomach rumbled a thanks when I didn't see any jellied sandwiches. I'd learned the hard way that I didn't want any food the UnSeelie had to offer, especially not from the Shadow man.

"Aren't you going to have a seat?" His lopsided grin only served to raise my hackles more. "There are plenty all around. Pick whichever you like."

"No, thank you. I think I'll stand." I tried to be discrete as I looked around, searching for an exit.

"Sit down, Katherine. It is rude to stand while the rest are seated." His eyes narrowed on me, a dark glint in his eyes.

"The rest—" I started, but the moment I questioned him, the other chairs at the table filled with dark figures. Each one a different shape and size. One of them vaguely looked rabbit shaped, and I dared not ask whom it was. Instead, taking the coward's way out, I took the seat at the opposite end that he had conveniently left empty for me.

"There." He clapped his hands together when I was where he wanted me. "Now, isn't that better?"

"What do you want?"

Frowning at me, he dropped his legs from the table and leaned forward on his elbows. "We have much to discuss, you and I."

"I don't have anything to say to you." I leaned forward on the table.

"Oh, we think you will want to know what we have to say." The reference to himself as a *we,* warned me that I was pissing him off enough that the Shadows contained in his corporeal form were getting agitated.

"Fine," I snapped. "But get rid of the freak show. You're not scaring anyone here."

I gestured to the shadowy forms that snapped their heads toward me.

"Now you've hurt their feelings." The Shadow man pouted, his lip protruding in a way that would have been adorable on anyone else, but not him. "Don't you want to see your friends? They so want to see you. They keep screaming it over and over again. It does give me a headache at times." He rubbed his temples to demonstrate his point.

"Then why don't you let them go?"

"Let them go? Why ever would I want to do that?" He stopped rubbing his head and leaned his cheek on one fist as his eyes lingered on the shadowy forms of those he had taken. "Besides, they came to me. I didn't force them to become part of my army. I offered them the same as I offered you."

"You mean you tricked them," I countered.

Just because they agreed didn't mean they knew what they were getting into. Who knew what it was like to be inside the Shadow man? Was it cold? Could they talk? Or were they squished together inside of that body, not able to move or breathe, just suspended there? Unable to die or break free. A shudder ran down my spine.

"No," he barked out. "We offered them love, acceptance, and power. Now they will get all those things and more. Just as you will when you join us. As our queen."

He held his hand out to me across the table, and I felt a new weight on my head and body.

Looking down, my dress from dinner with my mother had transformed into a spaghetti-strapped, silk dress the color of fresh blood. The neckline dipped down between my breasts, but somehow pressed my breast up, as if offering them to the viewer to have a taste. I reached my hand up to touch my head, bringing down a golden crown with enough jewels on it that even the richest man would envy.

While I was examining my new duds, the Shadow man found his way around the table and sat on bended knee next to my chair. He clasped my hand in his, bringing it to his chest so I could feel his beating heart. My skin revolted against me, trying to get away from the wretched feeling and leaving little pinpricks in their wake.

"Katherine, light of my life, freedom of my heart, I have loved you since the moment I saw you. Since you came back to our world. I couldn't imagine my life, or any life without you. Please make me the happiest Fae in the Underground by being the queen to my king. And I will make sure all of your needs and desires come true." As he spoke, his magic pressed down on me, drawing my gaze into his, and my body responded against my will. My heart beat faster and my mouth became dry. Neediness fell between my thighs, and they pressed together involuntarily.

I fought against the feeling of love he was forcing on my body and mind. I didn't love him, and I certainly didn't want him. I wasn't even sure he was able to feel love himself. All they were was hatred and loneliness. Love was so far from the feeling I would expect them to feel.

My mouth opened up to scream at him to go to hell, but I found myself with my back flat on the table, and the Shadow man looming above me. My eyes widened as a state of paralysis weighed down my limbs. Why wasn't my magic coming to my defense?

"I see you need convincing." His breath was hot on my skin. "We can be so very convincing."

Lying on top of the table with my hands limp at my sides, I couldn't do anything but watch when he slid his hand down the column of my neck. My insides screamed as his hand trailed from my neck and dipped down into the front of the dress he had put me in. I felt for my magic, commanding it to do something, anything, to get him away from me. But there was nothing. It was like it was never there to begin with, as if I wasn't there to begin with. That was when I remembered.

Of course, it wasn't here, because I wasn't really here. I was dreaming. He couldn't reach me in the human world, no matter whose magic he piggybacked onto. He didn't have the power to break through the wards separating the worlds. Not yet, anyway.

While I tried to keep from vomiting at the feel of his lips sucking on my collarbone, I did the only thing I could think of to get myself out of the dream. My hands wrapped around a fork on the table and stabbed it into the softest part of my thigh. My eyes pricked with tears, but the room and the Shadow man began to fade away. The anger on his face lingered in my mind, letting me know things between us weren't over.

CHAPTER 13

DANGEROUS

I JERKED AWAKE, my hand reached out beside me to find a cold, empty space next to me. Glancing down at the spot on the bed where Chess had been, I frowned. There wasn't a note or any indication of him ever being there. I placed my head in my hands to urge the Marti Gras parade jumping around in there to keep it down. It was worse than a hangover, and I wouldn't wish a power drain on my worst enemy.

At that thought, my eyes drifted to the mirror still hidden by the dark sheet. Goose bumps covered my arms just from thinking about what I had just been through. What was with people hijacking my dreams? It was bad enough I couldn't get away from the Fae in real life, now they had to make it their business to invade my quiet time too?

I hadn't even received any of the answers I needed.

And the Shadow man. What was with that proposal? As if a few pretty words and clothing would make me join them. If anyone could use a good dose of power hangover, it was the Shadow man. A big whopping bucket of hangover with a marching band stomping around to scramble his—their—brains.

I shook my head to clear out the weird spiral of crazy that I had launched into and slipped out of bed. I would have to be more careful with my thoughts. Maybe start taking some sleep inducers so I wouldn't dream at all.

Stretching out my aching limbs, I glanced at the alarm clock by my bed. Six thirty. I had plenty of time before I had to be at work. I kept a wide berth between the mirror and myself as I made my way around the bed. My eyes couldn't help but trail back to the empty spot on the mattress.

It was typical, really. What did I expect from a cat? They never followed directions, and they did whatever the hell they wanted to do, regardless of what others thought. I had let my expectations for Chess elevate to that of a normal human and, while he was becoming a good friend, I was finding it hard to trust him at times.

I walked into my bathroom and bypassed the mirror, knowing I probably looked like a crack whore who was in dire need of a fix and turned on the shower. I made sure the water made the bathroom nice and steamy before I stripped off last night's clothes and hopped into the almost scalding water.

The hot liquid soothed away my sore and aching muscles. While I had never experienced a power drain before, I hadn't imagined it would feel like this. Every inch of me felt like it had been run over by a Mac truck. My aches had aches, and though I didn't have any visible injuries, my insides had to be vibrant purple.

Just lifting my arms to wash my hair was a chore, and I thought about forgoing it all together, but every time I feel crappy, I always feel better when I look better. So clean, bouncy hair was a must.

Stepping out of the shower, I toweled my hair off before checking my face in the mirror. Not my normal fabulous complexion, but better than I hoped. I blinked once, and my eyes transformed to the glamoured green. I pursed my lips and had a sudden thought. My drab washed out skin faded into a healthy glow.

"Much better." I nodded to myself in the mirror and walked with a bit of pep in my step to my room.

I threw on a pair of jeans and one of my few nice tops, a pale lavender peasant top that tied at the base of my collarbone and flowed nicely over my hips. I slipped on my go-to, plain black flats and made my way to the kitchen.

When I entered, I stopped short at the sight of a teapot and cup sitting on the little table with a note leaning against it. Taking a cautious step forward, I glanced around the kitchen for any other changes but found none. Who could have left it? Chess?

Standing before the table, I picked up the note. 'Drink me' was all that was written on it in sharp but curvy handwriting that summed up Chess perfectly. Wonderful to look at, but might bite you if you try to pet him.

I sat down at the table and picked up the cooled cup. Bringing it up to my nose, I took a small sniff. A pungent aroma came from the liquid inside.

I jerked back and rubbed my nose to get rid of the smell from my nostrils. I didn't know much about medicines, especially not much of the herbal variety. Whatever was in the tea could be harmful to me, or it could be exactly what I needed, but I had no way of knowing for sure.

Moving from the table with the tea in hand, I made my way over to the sink. I stared down into the pit of the drain and contemplated pouring the tea out. On the one hand, Chess hadn't done anything that could be constituted as harmful. Perverted and slightly grabby, but certainly nothing on the lethal scale. Then again, everyone had been telling me not to trust him. Unfortunately, since none of them were willing to tell me why, I couldn't really count that as a viable reason. There was the chance that the tea might not even be from Chess in the first place, and then that meant I had a whole other set of problems with someone else being in my house.

As I fought back and forth in my mind on whether I should or shouldn't, my back door cracked opened. I really needed to start locking my house.

I tensed for what may lay behind the door. My shoulders sagged with relief seeing it was only Jewels. Then my relief was replaced with irritation.

"You know, it's called knocking. You should try it sometime," I growled, bringing the cup up to my mouth to take a sip of the most disgusting thing I had ever tasted in my life. My face must have portrayed how disgusted I was, because Jewels cocked his head, completely ignoring my complaint.

"What is that?" His nose wrinkled as if he could smell it from there, and for all I knew, he probably could. Even with my newly enhanced senses, my nose still probably wasn't as strong as a full-blooded Fae. A blessing in this situation.

"I think it's a hangover remedy." I looked down at the remaining tea in the cup, before setting it down. Not worth it.

Jewels moved across the room in that way only the Fae seemed to be able to do, as if their feet never touch the ground. I could see through his mesh shirt. The barbells in his nipples had been replaced with hoops with large, blood red gems. When I realized I was staring, I turned away from him and back to the sink.

"What does a princess need with a hangover remedy?"

I could feel his body heat as he stopped uncomfortably close to me, his voice just behind my ear.

I shrugged and turned back around to try to push him away a bit. "Not that it's any of your business, but it isn't really a hangover as much as a power outage."

171

Understanding filled his eyes. "Ah. Yes, they said that might be something that could happen."

I narrowed my eyes at his cryptic reply. "What could happen?"

He gave a nonchalant shrug, letting his blond hair curtain his face like he did when we were younger and he was hiding something. But then he peeked out from behind it with a sneaky smile on his face. For some reason, my skin crawled.

"Do you really want to know?" He tried to sound seductive, but it didn't work as well as it had in the ballroom. Not now that I remembered what he looked like in diapers, and I couldn't forget the little incident from our one and only date.

"Just tell me." I gave him a combination of my 'I'm a librarian and take none of your shit' and my recently recovered 'I can have your head in three seconds flat' glare.

He blew out an irritated breath. "Geez, you're no fun. I think I liked it better when you were just a silly little human."

"Well, I'm not just a silly little human. I'm your princess, and you will do as you are asked. What are they saying about me?"

"Hey, don't get your panties in a twist." He held his hands up in defense. "And it's kind of hypocritical to say you don't want to

172

be our princess, and then try to throw it in my face like that, don't you think?"

"Jewels," I ground out.

"Fine." The word snapped like a rubber band. I leaned back as he placed one hand on each side of the counter, effectively blocking me in. "You want to know what all the little Faelings are saying behind your back? You want to know what everyone is keeping from you?"

"Yes." I didn't yell at him to move back, afraid it would make him clam up when I was finally going to get some answers.

He leaned into me, close enough for me to see the pale lashes surrounding his eyes, and then without warning, I was drowning. My knees became weak, and my breath caught as his Fae mojo pressed down on me. I had only been on the receiving end of his and Dorian's pheromones a couple of times, and both times they hadn't been trying to do more than intimidate me. Jewels' had been more involuntary than Dorian's. But now that Jewels knew he could use it against me, he pushed it full force onto my human senses until I was a wobbly mess of hormones and need.

"You're dangerous," he whispered in my ear. A whimper leaked from my mouth. "A half-breed with full-blood power. No rules.

173

No limitations." His lips ghosted across my cheek, and he cupped my face in his hand, his full gaze pulsing into me. "Any moment, you could lose control. But if you had someone to answer to, someone that could control you..." He pulled my body flush against his, and then slid his hands down to my butt, slightly lifting me against him. My insides quivered at the feel of him while my mind screamed at me to break his hold. "Why, they'd be the most powerful being in this world and the next."

His mouth grazed mine, and my hands groped his shirt, twisting the fabric with my fists. His hand found the back of my head, and he angled my mouth to claim it, but just as his lips engulfed mine, my body caught up with my mind. I sent my knee straight up into his not so fun bags.

"Is it just me then?" a deep and bitter voice asked.

I tore my eyes away from the bent over bastard clutching his bruised manhood to find Dorian looming in the doorway. Did nobody knock anymore?

CHAPTER

JEALOUSY BECOMES HIM

I JUST COULDN'T catch a break. I looked back at Jewels and then to Dorian, my mouth gaping like a fish.

"This isn't what it looks like," I said. "He was—I was—"

"I do not wish to hear your excuses." Dorian's piercing eyes beat down on me, before turning to Jewels who had recovered from his injury. "You. What do you think you are doing here? Do you dare defy your queen's orders?"

Jewels stiffened, and with courage I didn't think the spineless asshole had, glowered in return, "I am doing as our queen instructed."

"I hardly believe molesting her daughter in broad daylight is what she had in mind when she—" He cut off mid-sentence as if remembering I was in the room.

"When she what?" I was over trying to defend myself to him. He, like everyone else, was hiding things from me. Important things.

"Nothing," he snapped, glaring at the smirking bastard next to me.

"Oh, I assure you, Lady, it is not nothing," Jewels goaded as if he hadn't just been on the receiving end of my knee. I owed him more than a swift kick in the junk and planned to pay up in full the next chance I got.

I turned on him. "Then you tell me."

Jewels opened his mouth, but before he could get a word out, he was clutching his own throat, an invisible hand lifting him off the ground to hover in the air.

"Tell her and lose your head, boy." The dark, threatening tone filled Dorian's voice, his hand tightened in the air, causing Jewels to make a gurgling noise.

"That's enough," I said. While the asshole deserved many things, strangulation and beheading being two of them, I didn't have the time or the patience to clean up a mess that big.

"You would defend this boy?" Dorian's eyes locked onto me, his anger bearing down on me. "Are your affections so easily tossed from one man to another, or does your human part simply open its legs to anyone?"

He did not just say that. I couldn't believe my ears or my eyes for that matter. He had not only walked in on me kneeing Jewels, which he didn't bother letting me explain, but he thought my human feelings were flighty?

I could sense my magic begin to wake beneath my skin. All feelings of weakness from last night's overload were gone in an instant. In its place were the telltale signs of my anger building itself into a fit of epic proportions. If he thought my destroying the kitchen was bad before, the things I could do now that I knew what I was doing—well, sort of knew what I was doing—I could wipe him off the face of the Earth with little more than a flick of my finger.

"How dare you," my voice came out low, dangerous, and full of power. "How dare you walk into my house and insult me. Talk as if I am not here and lie to my face."

"I—"

"I'm talking," I cut him off, using my powers to push him back a bit, breaking his connection to Jewels.

177

Jewels fell over, gasping. Then he stumbled forward and took off out the back door.

Coward.

With the bastard out of the way, it was just Dorian and I. Once again, like a few days ago, we were alone in my little kitchen about to fight. It seemed all we did was fight now. Though, I had been trying to keep my Fae life separate from my human one, it seemed parts of her kept creeping in. That part of me still wanted Dorian's approval.

I could remember a time where I thought we would never disagree. That we would always think as one, but back then I had assumed a lot of things. Thoughts of what we once were, what we once had, were like a bucket of ice water to my fiery anger.

It was easy for me to get angry, to act like he didn't matter, because those feelings weren't what they were anymore, but for him, they were as real as the day I died. They were etched on his soul as a reminder that he failed, and I was the price for that failure. Though it had been a misunderstanding, my forgiveness only went so far.

So instead of fighting, instead of letting my magic unleash upon my already beaten kitchen, I took a deep breath and let it out. I turned back to my tea. My disgusting, cold, tea that I was going to swallow every sip of if it killed me.

While I chugged the vile liquid, Dorian had the good smarts to keep silent, but his presence loomed in the background, ever present and alive. I couldn't forget him even if I wanted to.

I set down the now empty teacup.

"We can't keep doing this," I murmured and turned back to him, weariness in my eyes. "I can't keep doing this."

"You don't have to." He took two large steps over to me, grasping my hands in his. "Come back to the Underground. Where it is safe, and you can forget all of this." He waved his hand around the room. "You do not even have to go back to the Seelie Court. You could just come back to the UnSeelie Court. I am sure mother would be thrilled to have you amongst us."

I quirked my eyebrow at him.

"Or not," he added quickly. "You could stay anywhere. Anywhere you want. At Seer's or at that Opalaught's home. Just come back to us."

The thought of staying with Seer was not a pleasant one. While the blue skinned, blue haired pixie had her fair share of powers and would be better company than any troll, the thought of so many hands to watch out for kind of put a damper on things. Not to forget the constant smoking.

Trip, on the other hand, sounded like a better idea. I loved the little white devil, but he was one of those friends that you could only take so much in one setting before you needed to go away for a while. Far, far away.

Neither of the options would work, if I was even considering going back in the first place, which I wasn't.

"I don't mean I'm done being here." I removed my hands from his and locked eyes with him, to show how serious I was being. "I mean...this." I gestured between us. "Us."

"I do not understand." He tilted his head, his hair falling over the stagnant markings on his face, making him more handsome than ever.

"I know you don't, and that is the problem." I blew out an exasperated sigh. "I can't figure out who I am. Who I need to be with you here. Everyone wants me to come back."

"For your safety," he interjected.

"Right," I drawled out. "For my protection and because my mother doesn't want my unpoliced powers to get into the wrong hands. Which would be anyone but her."

Dorian eyes cast down at my revelation.

It didn't take a rocket scientist to figure out what she wanted. While beating the Shadows was all good and well, she wanted more than that from me. What she wanted that power for I didn't know, but I was sure it was more than I was willing to give.

"She only wants what is best for the kingdom, like she always has." Dorian's attempt to defend her would have been endearing had I not been trying to break up with him.

"My mother aside." I took a deep breath to steady my heart that was breaking by the minute. "I don't want to see you hanging around anymore."

"You do not want to see me?" His eyes filled with hurt and confusion and my aching heart sang for him.

"Not don't. Can't," I corrected myself. "Seeing you is hard. While I have forgiven you for what you did, I know it was a trick and everything; it doesn't change how I feel. How I felt. And having you here now, constantly trying to get me back when I don't know enough about me to know how I feel about anything, makes it that much harder."

"What are you trying to say, L—Kat?"

I smiled slightly at his catch. "See, you still see me as the girl you fell in love with. Even with a different face, you can't see past that. And while part of me does love you..." My chest ached a bit more when his eyes filled with joy. "That part is buried under all the baggage between us and the rest of the worlds. So, what I'm saying is that I need space."

He was quiet as he tried to comprehend my words. "Space?"

"Yes. Space."

"All right." He nodded his head. "I will keep my distance, but if that cat comes back I'll—"

"Do nothing because you won't be here," I interjected.

"Where will I be if not here?" He seemed genuinely confused as if the concept of giving me space was something he had never heard of.

"You will be home. In the Underground, spending time with your mother who you haven't seen in years and taking care of your realm," I offered up, hoping reminding him of his duties would somehow make what I was saying easier to swallow.

"And while I am there, you will be..."

"Here, in the human world, where I live."

He frowned hard. "But it is not safe here. What if the Shadows get over and come for you?"

"Then it is a good thing I am some all powerful half-breed, right? Plus, Chess will be here, and I highly doubt that will happen, anyway." I shrugged.

"So, that's it, is it?" His voice lost the understanding tone and turned malicious.

"What?" I stared up at him, confused.

"You just want me out of the way to be with him." He grabbed me by the shoulders, his grip bit into my skin. "Tell me, do you talk of all the Fae who have come to him as payment for his servitude? Do you curl up in your bed while he regales you with tales of his mass orgies?"

I gaped at him, not really believing the words that were coming out of his mouth. How could he flip suddenly from one emotion to the next? I had thought the spell on him was broken, and he would be his old charming self. Maybe the spell had only been a part of it, and this was the real him I saw now.

"Tell me what do I have to do to get you to give me a chance?" His grip was hurting now. He pulled me against him and jerked my face up to look into his eyes.

I knew what he was going to do the moment our eyes locked. I prepared for the pressure that came with his gaze, the pressure that was my body telling me he was trying to use his pheromones to control me. I hoped he wouldn't. I hoped I was right, that he was better than Jewels. I didn't push him away because a part of me wanted to know. Needed to know if he had fallen that far.

So, when my heart rate sped up and my thighs clenched, my heart sank into my stomach. I wasn't the only one who had changed. This wasn't my Dorian anymore. Either time, or the spell, had wrought their vengeance on him, and he was too weak of a Fae to resist the pull into insanity. I wanted to be angry with him. The logical side of me told me I should be, but all I felt was numb.

My magic shot a little spark out, enough to break his hold on me. He gaped and held his hands up in midair as if he couldn't believe I had stopped him. I took a step away from him and then another until I was at the kitchen door leading to the living room.

I gave him one last look, one that was full of regrets and wishes for happier times. And then all of the love that had lingered in my heart for the man I once knew faded away.

"Goodbye, Dorian."

I didn't have time for past loves. Or for regrets. All my focus had to be on the here and now. And the enemy I knew wasn't going to wait much longer for me to make my move.

CHAPTER

15

FUCKING FAERIES

THE MOMENT I stepped into the library at five past ten, Brandi was all over me.

"You're late." She crossed her arms over her primly pressed blouse, and her brows scrunched down as she frowned at me.

"I know. Sorry, time got away from me," I called over my shoulder as I passed by her to head to the main circulation desk. I could feel Brandi's eyes drilling holes in my back as I put my bag up and clocked in. I waited for her to say her piece.

"If that boyfriend of yours is making you late, you might want to rethink your priorities before you don't have a job to come back to."

I looked over to where Mrs. Jenkins was already set up at her computer and rolled my eyes before turning back to Brandi. "I'll get right on that."

Apparently, I didn't hide my sarcasm well enough, because her frown deepened and then morphed into a smirk. "David called in sick, so you're on nonfiction today."

I tried to suppress my groan.

The library was broken up into four sections. The main circulation desk, which was the first and last place people saw as they maneuvered the library. Usually, Mrs. Jenkins and I worked that desk. It was the busiest part of the library, and usually, that meant time went by quicker. With Mrs. Jenkins as my wing woman, it made the day just a little bit more bearable and a lot more entertaining.

After the main desk was the children's section, where a petite brunette named Tammy worked. She had a sweet smile and more patience than the Pope. I hadn't really ever thought of having children, but just walking by the children's section would deter me from having them anytime soon.

The second floor wasn't quite as busy as the first floor, since all the fiction books and movie rentals were downstairs. This floor had the computer center where a nerdy guy with glasses that spent way too much time at the gym worked. I hadn't gotten his name yet. He kind of kept to himself, and really, he just freaked me out. If you'd ever seen him catch someone trying to watch porn on the library's Internet you would be scared too.

Beside the computer center, there was the Teen Center, where all the manga and young adult books lived. They also had a closed off room for teen nights and had video games and Magic card fights. I wished they'd had that kind of stuff when I was a teen, then again, I probably wouldn't have come, anyway. People and such. But being in the teen section was only the second place you didn't want to end up. Who wanted to referee a bunch of horny, rambunctious teens?

Lastly, there was the nonfiction desk. Technically it was in the middle of the second floor between the computer center and the teen center with the nonfiction section split up around the rest of the space. But for lack of imagination, we called it the nonfiction desk.

No one liked working that desk. Why? Because it was boring as fuck. Unless you got a huge influx of students needing a reference for their school project, which never happened with the card system on the computer, you pretty much sat there twiddling your thumbs and catching up on your reading. The occasional cart of books would need to be shelved, but that was the most excitement you could expect from it. Which was the exact amount of excitement I gave Brandi.

"Who's going to help Mrs. Jenkins? Can't what's his face watch both?" I gave her a closed mouth smile, hoping to get out of it.

"No," she snapped. "Henry cannot watch both. He has a hard enough time with the section he has. Besides, could you imagine him working with actual people?" She didn't wait for my response before continuing, "That is a lawsuit waiting to happen. I will help Mrs. Jenkins today, and you can handle nonfiction since you have so much on your mind to think about nowadays."

"Great." I hoped she didn't hear the sarcasm dripping from my words. I gave Mrs. Jenkins an apologetic smile and mouthed good luck.

She shooed me away. "Don't you worry about me, girl. I've been managing this desk for years even without help. I'll catch up with you later, and you can tell me all about this new boyfriend the boss lady here has been droning on about."

A smile crept up onto my face, but I stifled it when Brandi shot Mrs. Jenkins a warning look. Apparently, Chess had left an impression, and a big one, at that. Too bad he was nowhere to be found. I could have used his help this morning. Though, with the way things were going, he might have been more hindrance than help.

I grabbed my bag and phone and pointed a thumb toward the stairs. "Well, I'm going to head up then. If you need anything, you know where I'll be."

But all that didn't compare to having to work the front desk with Brandi. I would rather be bored out of my mind than listen to her drone on about the latest gossip going on in her little clique. I was lucky to have gotten away without her making some back ass comment about my eyes being back to normal. I could only hope that I could keep the glamour up, and no magical hiccups would come my way.

Though, several long and torturous hours later, I was dying for a magical hiccup. I was so bored. You would think in a library full of books, I would be able to find something to keep me entertained in between shelving, and the rare and random reader needing help finding something, but that wasn't the case. When you were basically living a fairy tale, it was hard to get into anything else.

So, after lunch, when I couldn't take it anymore, I found myself in the self-help section. I was bound to find something I could use against my mother—my Fae mother, that was—that would help me stay in the human world while helping her do whatever it was she wanted me to do.

I pulled a few books off the shelf, like *How to Win Any Argument* and *Manipulation 101*, and made my way to the law section to freshen up on moderators and verbal agreements. I'd already paid my dues to Teeth, but I had promised the Shadow man to come back. I needed some leverage on how to go about completing that agreement.

On my way to the law books, I passed the medical section where I stopped when there was a giggle followed by a moan. Great. Just what I needed. I wanted some action, and now I got it. The words *be careful what you wish* for definitely came into play here.

Setting my books down on the nearest table, I prepped myself for what I was about to do. No one liked to be that person. The party pooper who had to break up all the fun with logic and societal rules. I was all for having fun, especially the recreational orgasm inducing kind. But I had never been the adventurous type when it came to sex in public places. Give me a soft bed and easy access to a bathroom for clean up any day.

"God, please let them have their clothes on," I muttered before rounding the corner of where the sound was coming from.

My eyes half closed in case I came face to face with someone's butt, or worse, the full Monty, I cleared my throat. Through my eyelashes, I saw an attractive couple, both thankfully clothed, but just a few seconds away from being on top of each other. The girl gave a little squeal. She turned away to, I assumed, put her bra back into place.

"What the hell, man?" The guy asked as he buckled his belt. "Couldn't you have, you know, just ignored us?"

"Just ignored you?" I crossed my arms over my chest, my eyes fully open as I took them in. "You have to be what? Seventeen?"

"Nineteen." The boy smirked, so proud of his age.

Only a little bit older, and I already felt like an old woman. Even in Fae years, I was still a baby at a century-and-a-half.

"And you?" I eye the girl that didn't look older than fifteen.

The girl hesitated, before quietly saying, "Sixteen."

192

Frowning hard, I glared at the two. "And you thought the library was a good place to what? Commit statutory rape?"

"Hey!" The nineteen-year-old stepped up to me, trying to intimidate me with his height. "What we do is none of your business, lady." He grabbed his girlfriend's hand, giving her a loving smile. "Besides, it's called the Romeo and Juliet clause. Look it up."

He glared at me before pulling the girl out of the aisle.

I stood there shocked that the boy could be so loving one moment and then nasty the next. All these flip flop emotions were giving me whiplash. I had a hard enough time controlling my own, let alone dealing with others.

I shook my head, wondering if I should have minded my own business when my eye caught what section we were in. Right there, plain as day, was a sign for sexually transmitted diseases. I started to laugh so hard, I had to put my hand on the shelf to catch myself. It wasn't really that funny.

With a little bit more pep in my step, I made my way back to my pit of despair. I opened up one of the books I had grabbed and started looking through the index for anything that might help me. A moment later the sixteen-year-old stepped up to my counter.

Glancing up to the blushing teen, I waited for her to speak up.

"I'm sorry about Jeremy." She thumbed back to where her boyfriend was waiting by the stairs with a scowl on his face. "He's just upset because I haven't told my dad about us yet. He really is a good guy." She got that dreamy look on her face that I remembered getting whenever I used to think about Dorian. The very thought of him made my little bit of pep die.

"Do you love him?" I inquired, staring down the boy until he finally glanced away. I smirked inwardly at my small victory.

"Yeah." If possible, she blushed even more.

"And he loves you?"

"Oh, totes!" Her face lit up like the red light district after nine o'clock. It was contagious, and I felt myself beginning to smile in return.

"Then there's no problem. Love may not conquer all, but don't let a silly thing like age or your parents' approval stand in your way." I patted her hand and turned back to my book.

She gave me a huge smile and skipped away.

I almost let it go, but then the little punk boyfriend flipped me the bird.

"And use a condom," I called out.

The few patrons on the floor turned to us, and both the teens bowed their heads and hurried away.

Having done my good deed for the day, I spent the next few hours buried in legalese. By the time eight o'clock rolled around, I felt like my head was full of gibberish. While I had gone to college, nothing prepared me for the extensive terminology from one of the books I had picked up. I had never felt as stupid as I had right then. I had to use a dictionary just to keep up with what they were saying. Maybe if I just threw a few big words at my mother and the Shadow man, I'd confuse them enough to get out of it?

With my arms loaded with books, I made my way downstairs to the main desk where Mrs. Jenkins sat as happy as could be with Brandi nowhere in sight. Giving a curious glance around, I placed my books on the counter and handed her my card.

"Where's the Queen B?" I asked, making sure I put plenty of emphasis on the B part.

Mrs. Jenkins gave a deep chuckle and set about scanning my books out. "That girl didn't last half the day before she snuck away for a business call, and she hasn't come out of the office since." She snorted. "She wouldn't know how to do real work if it bit her in that perfectly lypo'd ass."

"Mrs. Jenkins! Such language," I cried out in mock shock. "Well, I hope it wasn't too bad down here on your own."

I gave her a worried look.

Stacking my books into a neat pile, she shook her head. "Now, don't you be worrying about little old me. You have bigger things to worry about."

"Like what?" I cocked my head, wondering what she could know that I didn't.

"Like that boyfriend of yours, and this identity crisis you seem to be having." She gestured to my blonde hair. "You shouldn't be changing who you are for the sake of those around you."

I grabbed some of my hair and frowned. "I didn't really do it on purpose. It kind of just happened. And he's not my boyfriend."

Mrs. Jenkins' dark eyes narrowed. "Says him? Or you?"

"Both. Neither." I sighed. "We aren't together like that."

"But you'd like to be." This time, her eyes had a knowing gleam to them.

I picked up my books and held them to my chest, trying to think it out. "I don't know. Maybe. I guess. It's complicated."

"Isn't it always?" She chuckled, shaking her head. "Girl, you have a good head on your shoulders, but sometimes you think too much with your big brain and not enough with your lady parts."

"What?" I choked out, thinking I'd heard wrong.

"You heard me. From what I know, this boy of yours is a tasty little morsel, and if you don't grab him up, the boss lady or someone else will gobble him up before you can figure out what you want."

"Just because I lust after him doesn't mean we should be together," I pointed out.

"Well, it's as good a starting point as any." She shrugged. "Life is too short to not take any risks. You might not love him, but if you can tolerate him long enough to get a few orgasms out of it, I say why not take the chance? You might be surprised at what you find out about him and yourself."

Speechless, I could only nod in response. I turned away from the desk and started for the door, my head full of too much information and weirdness for one day.

"And Kat."

"Yes?" I turned back as she made her way around the counter.

She rubbed her arms as if she were cold and glanced up at the skylight where the night sky could be seen, and where the half moon was shining.

"You watch yourself out there tonight. I have a bad feeling something's coming. Something big." Her eyes locked onto mine. The dark lines on her face deepened as if she were aging this very moment. "And you will be the center of it."

I gaped at her, but couldn't take anymore. I marched out of the library, dead set on getting home. The more I knew about magic and Fae, the more I seemed to find it all around me. Who else could have Fae blood in them? And how long until they were released upon this world?

I made my way to my car, keeping my eyes straight ahead and my keys poised and ready. No sooner had my eyes landed on my car, then I felt it. Something in the air that had the distinct feeling of magic.

I gave a cursory glance around but didn't see anything until I heard it. Buzzing. Like a dozen tiny wings beating in unison. I didn't wait to see it. I took off for my car.

My feet pounded on the ground, and my heart thundered against my chest. A familiar war cry called out behind me and tiny hands jerked at my hair. Not letting it deter me, I covered my head with the books and kept going, their laughter piercing my ears.

Fucking faeries.

The buzzing had been wings. Faerie wings. And by the looks of it, the whole fucking horde that had attacked me back in the Veil of the Faeries was here.

They flitted around me, surrounding me on all sides. Dark brown bodies with black hair and even blacker eyes laughed at me. Their thin veiny wings beat behind them as they tried to take me down. I would have thought after my last encounter with the little devils they'd have learned not to mess with me, but it looked like they needed another lesson.

Spinning around on them, I locked eyes with their leader. The faeries jerked on my hair and clothes, their attacks more to irritate than to cause harm. I wasn't fooled. They seemed harmless to those who didn't know their game, but I wasn't waiting around for them to turn those sharp teeth on me.

As I called on my magic, and as the feel of it crept onto my skin, a small look of fear made them hesitate. So they did remember. Good.

Hoping against hope that the magic would do what I wanted, I pushed it to form a bubble around me. Before they could retreat, I shoved it at them causing their tiny bodies to spin away from me with a chorus of screams.

The moment they weren't surrounding me, I flew the last few feet to my car. I jerked open the door and dove inside. Just as I slammed the door shut, several thuds smacked against the window. They sure as hell rebounded fast.

"What the fuck?" I whispered to myself.

How did they get here? Why were they here? Mrs. Jenkins wasn't wrong when she said something was coming, and if these little pests got out of the Underground, there was no telling what else was on its way. I just hoped the world was ready for them, because I sure as hell wasn't.

CHAPTER 16

ALICE

AS I MADE my way home, pedal to the metal became my new motto. I drove like hell itself was on my heels, and with faeries in the human world, that very well could have been the case.

When I pulled into my driveway, I didn't get out right away. I held my breath, waiting to be attacked once more by flying twigs. When no attack seemed to be coming, I clicked off my car and took a cautious step out. The moment my feet hit the ground, I booked it for the house, not relying on the chance that I might have lost them for good.

I unlocked my door and threw myself inside. My heart beat like a rampant drum as I pushed the door closed and put the lock back in place. Backing away from the door, I took deep calming breaths and tried to get ahold of myself.

There were faeries in the human world. Okay. I could deal with this. It's not like I didn't deal with Fae every day. But why were they here? What would happen when the word spread that there were creatures not of this world running amuck? There would be something on the news by now, wouldn't there?

I turned to switch on my grandmother's only television, a small 32" flat screen that was in dire need of an upgrade, only to smack right into a warm, hard body.

Repressing a scream, I lashed out to attack whoever was in my home.

"Stop. Stop. Don't hurt me," a bell-like voice cried out. A voice I recognized and never thought I'd hear again.

I rushed to the light and flipped it on to reveal Alice Liddell. Her blonde hair was tied back with a blue bow, and her bright blue eyes, filled with unshed tears as they bore down on me. Her usually glamoured dress was back to its old ragged one. Her arms and legs were covered in dirt and scratches as if she had been running through the forest.

"Alice?" I blinked. "What are you doing here?"

"You have to help me." She reached out to me, grabbing my arms. "Please. You have to hide me."

"Hide you? From who?" I shook my head. "Wait. Why are you even here? *How* are you even here?"

Her blue eyes widened in surprise. "You don't know?"

"Know what?" Even as I asked the question, my heart sank into my stomach. Faeries and Alice? It could hardly be a coincidence.

"The doors," she stuttered out as if afraid to talk about it.

"What about them?"

"They're open." Her voice was hushed as if it was a great secret to be kept—and it was.

The doors between the human world and the Fae world were locked tight and could only be opened by a key, a key that had to be issued to you by the secretary in your respective court. No one got in or out without a key. The sister bird heads usually saw to that.

"What about the sisters? Aren't they supposed to be in charge of guarding the doors?" I knew the answer before she even said it.

"Gone. Poof. Into thin air." She let go of my arms and flopped down on the couch, grabbing a tissue from the box on the table in front of her to dab her face. "One day the door was just gone and so were they. No one knows what happened, and everyone has gone insane. Well, more insane than they normally are."

"Wait, you said the doors were open, not gone."

"Same thing, really." She shrugged and blew her nose in an unbelievably ladylike fashion.

"And when you say gone, you mean...?" I sat down next to her, hoping to drag more information out of her.

"Completely blown off their hinges!" Her voice was full of horror, and it made me want to see it for myself, but the thought of leaving my house anytime soon made my palms sweat and a feeling of light-headedness come over me. It wasn't safe out there for anyone, least of all me.

"Does the Queen know about this? Shouldn't she have guards on the door to keep people from getting out?"

"Well, of course, she knows, silly, and there are guards there. Not that they do much good, anyhow. The faeries blew right by them and out the door before they could even blink." She gave a small sneaky smile. "I snuck out with them while the guards were trying to contain them. One benefit of my glamour."

"So why are you here then? Why come back at all?" I didn't understand how she could throw her human life away so easily to be a Fae and now come back after all this time.

My question must have struck something in her, because she began to cry again. I grabbed the box of tissues and handed them to her, patting her on the back in a there-there kind of manner. Crying women weren't my forte, even being a woman myself.

"It's okay. You're safe here," I said. "You can tell me what happened."

"It's...it's just awful." She hiccupped. "When they found out I had been freed, and that the Shadows were on the loose as well, they came to the conclusion that I had something to do with it. Which is ridiculous!" She jumped up from her seat. "I was stuck in that mirror until you came and released me. You and the Shadow man." She stopped in front of me, pointing a finger at me, her voice filled with accusation, "You!"

You did this. You let them take corporeal form. It should be you they are after, not me!"

"I didn't let them do anything," I snapped, standing. "They tricked me. I have nothing to do with what is going on now. I've been here the whole time. I don't even know what has happened to my own friends. How can I be responsible for the whole Underground?"

"But you are! Don't you see?" She grabbed me by the arms. Her eyes locked me in place. "You are the only one capable of being responsible for them. The only one powerful enough."

"That's ridiculous." I shook her hands off me. "I can barely keep my glamour up, let alone control a whole other world."

"I could teach you," she offered, eagerness to please in her eyes.

"Not like I haven't heard that before." Everyone thought they could teach me. Everyone thought that I could save them. I couldn't even save myself.

"But I must give something in return for keeping me safe," she insisted.

"No. You don't." I sighed, rubbing my head. "This is the human world. You don't have to give something to get something. It doesn't work like that. You should remember that much."

Alice had been human once upon a time, until she fell in love with a neighbor boy called Lewis. He stole her stories of Wonderland for his book and broke her heart. She turned to Fae magic for help, and in turn, caused a series of events that led to my own demise and her imprisonment. Now she was like me. A half-blood, only not, since her powers were given to her by a mysterious tree with glowing fruit that liked to talk in cryptic riddles. I still had to figure out what was going on with that one.

"But can I still stay here?" She glanced around distaste on her face. "With you?"

"Sure." I threw my hands up in defeat. "Why not? Here, follow me. I'll show you the guest room."

I led her down the hall to one of the few rooms in the tiny house and opened the door, flicking the light switch on and gesturing inside.

"There are linens in the closet and towels in the bathroom, which is down the hall." I pointed out the bathroom door. "My room is over there, so if you need anything, let me know. Feel free to eat what you want from the kitchen, but be wary, there are a few iron pots I have yet to dispose of. Any questions?"

I watched her face as she took in the tiny room with the small double bed and simple decorations. She stepped inside and spun around in place. When she stopped a few emotions ran across her face, most of them unpleasant, before she gave me a polite smile.

"Well, I believe I will bid you goodnight." She stopped for a moment and glanced down at her dirty clothes and back to the clean bed. "I don't suppose you —"

"Have something you can wear? Sure." I took the few steps to my room and grabbed the top shirt and shorts in my drawers and handed them to her. "Here. Anything else?"

Taking the clothes in her hands, she hugged them to her. "No, I think I'm all right."

"Good. Well, I don't know about you but I'm pooped, so I'm heading to bed." I stretched to show my exhaustion.

"All right," she said slowly. I turned away to go back to my room, but she called out, and I forced myself not to groan.

"Yes?"

"Thank you. Really. You do not know how much this means to me."

My eyebrows rose in surprise at her words. I hadn't expected that from her of all people. Alice was more self-entitled than any royal I knew, and I knew plenty. Or, well, I did.

"You're welcome." I nodded back to her.

"Even if it is all your fault," she muttered after me.

I didn't respond since she was right. It was my fault, and the guilt was eating me alive. I didn't know what to do or where to start to fix my problem. For more than once that day, I wished Chess were here. He'd know what to do.

CHAPTER

CATS AND TROLLS

MY FINGERS TANGLED in the long tresses of the figure above me, the soft texture like silk against my fingertips. My body shuddered when the ends tickled my stomach and breasts with each movement. The caresses were a delightful contrast to the sharp nips of his canines as he made his way down my midsection.

My head fell back, and a gasp ripped from my throat as he settled between my thighs. Ricochets of pleasure tore through my body, and my hips bucked up to meet him. A growl reverberated through me in return, and I spilled over the edge.

"Chess!" I cried out and jerked up from the bed with a gasp, the orgasm startling me from my dream.

I groaned and rubbed my hand over my face before I collapsed back onto my pillow. I lay there, basking in the best sex dream I'd ever had. My mind tried to rationalize why I would even be dreaming about the sexy feline. I felt eyes boring into me.

A growl rumbled across the room, and my eyes locked onto the very Fae I had been dreaming about.

His crystal green eyes were bright in the shadows of my room, in the way only someone with a magical essence could pull off. His body and face were hidden by the darkness. The single window in my bedroom allowed only a tiny bit of light from the moon. While my eyesight was still slowly trying to adjust, the intensity of his gaze as it spread across my upper torso which was barely hidden beneath my thin tank top, made my skin tingle.

Pulling the sheet up over my top half, I cocked my head.

"Chess?" I cleared my throat, trying to get the breathy sound out of my voice as I sat up straighter in bed.

His eyes slid down my sheet-covered chest as if he could see right through it. The remnants of my dream still had me aching, and his attention wasn't making it any easier to forget. I tried to think of something else, anything else, so as not to give away my need.

"What were you dreaming about, my decadent kitty Kat?" His voice purred as he unwrapped himself from his seat by the wall.

My gaze fell on him as he moved further into the light of the room. All thoughts fled my mind. His hair swept across his bare chest, resting just above his navel. His pants hung low on his hips, the material tight and form fitting, showing all of the strength in his thighs. The vision he made was close enough to the dream version of him that it had parts low inside me tightening in remembrance.

He slithered onto my side of the bed, and I fought the urge to move away from the feral look in his eyes. Chess slid his hand along the length of my arm, sending a trail of heat over my skin in its wake. I couldn't repress a shiver as that hand moved from my arm to slip around my neck, and then up to cup my face in his hands.

I found myself leaning into his touch, the need to have him close too strong to ignore. My eyes fluttered closed, and I let myself enjoy his touch a little bit more. He moved in closer, leaning his top half over mine.

"I think I know what you were dreaming about." His mouth hovered above mine, brushing so lightly against it before nipping at my bottom lip. I leaned in as he pulled away. "I want to hear you say it."

I moaned at his teasing words. As his hands found their place on either side of me, my senses filled with nothing but his heady scent. My hand reached up tangling itself in his hair, his strands were just as soft as in my dream. I imagined what they'd feel like against my hot skin.

"Tell me, kitten, and I'll give you what you want," he purred against my throat as he arched my neck to the side, exposing my throat to him.

He bit at the junction where my neck and shoulder met, and my breath caught in my throat. With a smile, he slid his hand up the line of my thighs.

"You," I croaked out, unable to hold back anymore.

"Yes? What about me?" He teased, his smile pressing against my skin.

"I was dreaming about you," I shoved out as I fought to keep my hips on the bed and to keep from forcing his hands where I needed them most.

"Hmmm. And did you miss me, Kat? While I was gone? Or were you too wrapped up in your prince to notice?" His grip tightened on me, the hard sound of his voice was like a splash of cold water to my libido, and I jerked away from him.

"No," I snapped at him, irritated at my own lack of self-control. "And stay out of my head."

He gave me an amused smile. "Sadly, dream manipulation has never been one of my gifts, but I did partake in one of Seer's more interesting gatherings. Mass daydreams can be so satisfying when in the right setting."

My lips twisted down at the thought of a bunch of Fae sitting around getting high and having mental orgies. I'd been on the receiving end of one of her vision quests, and it didn't leave me satisfied in the least.

Changing the subject, I drew the covers up around me. "Where were you?"

"Working. Where else?" He shrugged as if it was an everyday occurrence.

"But you left." I winced at the desperation in my voice. "You weren't here and..."

My voice broke and all the events of the last few days caught up with me. Tears fell down my face and racking sobs filled my chest.

I curled my hands into fists and clenched the covers to me while trying to hide the agony on my face. My chest felt heavy and full of so many emotions I couldn't keep them in any longer, but I was never a pretty crier. My face would get blotchy and my nose red and puffy, so much so that I turned my face away from Chess to try to hide it.

"Shh." He ran his hand through my hair and then stroked my back. "If I had known you would be this upset, I would have woken you first, or at least left a note. Know that I didn't leave because I wanted to."

"Then why?" I asked in a small voice, coated with tears.

"A messenger came, and there was business that needed my attention. I didn't think you would care." His words had a slightly bitter tone to them.

"I do care," I retorted. "I mean. We're friends. I would want to know if you were going to be in danger."

His cat-like eyes watched me for a moment before he spoke. "Right. Friends. And how is that working out for us?"

I opened my mouth to answer, to say we were fine, but snapped it shut. We weren't fine. We weren't even close to fine. The world was falling apart, and I still couldn't admit that I wanted the Fae in front of me, because of pride, or plain old stubbornness.

Mrs. Jenkins' words echoed through me. I might not love Chess, but I knew I liked him. I missed him when he was gone. When there was a problem, I thought of what he would do, and like it or not, I was jealous of the other Fae who had been in his bed. And God help me, I wanted him. I wanted him more than anything in this world or the next. I didn't know much about anything else in my crazy life, but I did know that.

Chess moved away, and I could physically see him closing himself off from me. I had a feeling if that happened; I wouldn't ever get this chance back. If I wanted him, it had to be now.

"We're not." I grabbed his wrist, stopping him from leaving. "Friends, that is."

He glanced down at my hand and back to my face, a cautious look in his eyes. "Then what are we?"

I pulled him down to me and muttered, "Hell if I know," before pressing my mouth to his.

Chess didn't hesitate to cup the back of my head and press me closer to him. Angling my head slightly, I opened my mouth to him and let his slightly rough tongue slide in. Kissing someone with feline

216

qualities, like sharper canines, was a slight challenge. You couldn't really go crazy unless you wanted a tongue piercing. Since I didn't, I let Chess take the lead and found myself so consumed in our kiss that I didn't realize he had laid me back onto the bed until I felt him pressed between my legs.

I pulled back from the kiss with a gasp and then let out a slight groan. We were moving so fast. I mean, I wanted this, but I wasn't sure I wanted this right now. Not with everything that was going on. Especially since I just admitted to myself that I craved him.

"What is it?" He leaned back, watching my face, his eyes still full of desire. "I thought you wanted this."

"I did. I do," I explained, a blush filling my face. "Its just there is so much happening, I don't know if it would be right. Or if it would even be me doing this because I wanted to, or me being so overwhelmed. You know with the Shadows loose, Fae going missing left and right. Then there are the faeries and Alice being in the human world. You know what I mean?"

"Faeries? Alice? Here?" He pulled back as if I had bit him. He stood from the bed and started for the door. "Why didn't you tell me?"

217

"I was so distracted by the fact that you were actually back, that I forgot." I pushed away from the bed to go after him. I placed my hand on his arm, stopping him before he could open the door. "And then we were a little preoccupied."

A silly grin filled my face at what had just happened.

He pressed his lips to mine in a soft kiss. "Yes, that we were. But for once, and I cannot believe I am saying this, there are more pressing matters than consummating our new non-friendship."

"You're right."

Chess' eyes darkened. "If Alice and the faeries are here, than others may follow. Others that may want to take matters into their own hands. I have to go back and take care of a few things, make some preparations."

"The Fae are already through, what else is there to prepare for?"

"For all hell to break loose."

Glass shattered behind me as if it'd been waiting for Chess to say those words. I spun around and backed up. My bedroom window had been smashed and was now a big gaping hole. The frame around it had been ripped apart, and in its place, a burly figure loomed over us.

"What is that?" I took a step back, my back bumping into the wall behind me.

Chess tensed up beside me, his eyes focused on the creature. "That, my dear, is a troll."

"That's a troll?" I pointed at what looked to be a supersized man on steroids, with a pig snout for a nose and tusks coming out of his mouth. It wore only a flap over its private areas and dragged a large club behind it, which it now waved in the air with a roar.

"Are you all right in there?" Alice's voice chimed in from behind the door before the doorknob rattled.

"We're fine. Don't come in here." I called out to her. I didn't know what would happen if the troll saw Alice, especially since the rest of the Underground hated her guts. Luckily for me, she actually listened to me this time and moved away from the door.

With Alice gone, Chess leaned over and whispered, "He might not look like much, but believe me, love, you don't want to be getting on this guy's bad side. They're stupid but strong as hell."

Once the troll was done with his war cry, his tiny eyes looked around my room, as if he was a child in a toy store. Not paying us any mind, he stomped his large feet over to a line of rag dolls my grandmother had on display on the dresser.

"What is he doing?" I kept my voice down, trying not to draw the troll's attention.

"I don't know." Chess shrugged. "Why don't you ask him?"

"What?" I scoffed. "I can't do that, he'll eat me!"

"That's silly. Trolls don't eat beautiful ladies." Chess smirked at me.

My eyes narrowed in a scowl. How was I supposed to know what trolls ate? I'd never seen one before now. Everything I had ever learned about trolls was from fairy tales. They normally lived under bridges and required you to answer a riddle to get by, but this guy didn't look like he could spell his own name, let alone spout out a riddle.

"Excuse me." I cleared my throat and took a hesitant step forward, but the troll's attention securely focused on the doll he was playing with. I tried again a bit louder this time. "Excuse me."

The troll glanced toward me with a curious expression, as if he hadn't known I was even there.

"Hi." I gave a small wave. "That's a nice doll you have there." I pointed to the doll in his hand with a smile. "That belonged to my grandmother, but she's gone right now, so you could have it if you want."

He looked to the doll and back to me, clearly confused at the concept.

"It's a gift," I offered up, hoping he would know what that meant.

"Gift?" it said in a voice that sounded like he had been gargling rocks.

"Yes. A gift."

He looked down at the doll, and then to me. When his gaze slid over to Chess, he scowled. "Why?"

I stepped in front of Chess, trying to bring his focus back to me. I didn't know what his beef was with Chess, but he was talking and not destroying things, and I wanted to keep it that way.

"Because we are friends." I smiled up at him.

"Friends?" He pointed at himself and then at me.

"Yep. Friends. So as your friend, I have to ask, why did you come through my window?" I gestured toward the hole in my wall.

The troll looked back toward the hole as if not remembering he had been the one to create it. He scratched his head, and I could see him struggling to remember.

221

"Did you come to see me?" I asked.

"You?" He tilted his head to the side. "Who you?"

"I'm Kat." I placed my hand on my chest. "Who are you?" I was beginning to feel kind of silly having to dumb down everything I said, but if it kept him happy, I'd even go so far as interruptive dance to get the big lug out of my house.

"Bar," was his delighted reply.

I raised my eyebrow at the name but didn't question it. "Well, it is nice to meet you, Bar. Do you remember why you came here? To the human world?"

"Humans?" He tensed up, his eyes on alert. "Where humans?"

Knowing I was going to regret it, I held my hands up. "I'm a human, Bar. And this is Chess, the moderator."

I gestured to Chess behind me.

"Moderator!" The troll roared, his hand tightening around the doll. He stomped his feet, causing the whole house to shake. "Bar not bad! Not bad."

Chess stepped out from behind me, his hands on his hips. "I am not here for you, you big lug. But I might be if you don't stop playing games and tell us why you busted in here."

Suddenly it was like the lights went on in the troll's head. Before it was a dim bulb that made me think he had been dropped one too many times as a child, but now there was intelligence there. But also fear.

"The queen wants the human. The queen ask Bar to get human."

Of course, it was my mother who sent him. I knew she wanted power but to go this far was getting ridiculous.

Chess seemed to figure it out as well and stood in front of me. "The queen will have to wait. I need the human right now."

"But the queen." A tiny quiver filled Bar's voice.

"The queen can answer to me," Chess' voice rang with authority that had my insides tingling. "You can go back and tell her what I said, and if she tries to punish you, I will see to it."

The troll hesitated. Chess obviously had more pull than I thought he did, even if he wasn't exactly the moderator anymore.

"Go!" Chess' voice rang out throughout the room.

The troll scrambled back out the way he came, his hands clutching the doll I had given him.

When he was gone, I sighed as I took in the damage to my grandmother's house.

How the hell was I going to explain this? I dragged my hand through my hair and set to work on picking up broken pieces of the wall and putting them into a pile.

"Your mother is getting out of hand."

"Yeah," I muttered, focusing on not getting cut by the shards of glass littering the floor.

"All the more reason I need to go."

My head jerked up. "Go? Now? After I just got attacked? What if he comes back?"

Chess placed his hands on my shoulders and rubbed them in a soothing manner. "You'll be fine. He won't come back, believe me."

"But why was he more scared of you than my mother? You're not even the moderator anymore." I leaned into his embrace, accepting his comfort.

"I might not be the moderator anymore, but I still have a certain pull in the Underground. And like you, my power isn't limited by rules." He placed his chin on top of my head and stroked my hair. "What worries me is how he got out in the first place?"

I leaned back to see his face. "From what Alice said, the guards aren't that good at their job, but since he said my mother sent

224

him, I have no doubt that he was probably let out."

"Which is also a huge problem." Chess placed his clawed finger under my chin, tipping my head further back. "I won't let anything happen to you. Not while I'm around, but since I won't be for the next few days, you need to keep alert to your surroundings. Don't leave the house for anything other than your job and make Alice pull her weight around here. She might make a horrible Fae, but she still has more control over her magic than you do."

"I'm not a child. I can take care of myself." I pouted.

He nipped at my lip with a grin. "I am well aware of that."

His hands slid their way down my hips and pulled me close. My heart rate sped up.

My eyes fluttered closed as he dipped his head down. His lips engulfed mine, and I opened my mouth to him, savoring his kiss. Each sweep of his tongue caused my insides to light on fire and soon my hands found their way to his shoulders. I pushed myself up on my tiptoes to get closer to him. Just as his hands began to trail further down my hips, the bedroom door slammed open, revealing Alice's horrified expression.

"What in the name of all that is good happened here?"

* * *

AFTER CHESS LEFT, leaving me aching to continue where we had left off, I explained to Alice what had gone down. When that was done, I wanted nothing more than to go back to bed but that wouldn't happen until I fixed the new hole in my wall.

I found a piece of plywood big enough to cover the hole, and though it wasn't the prettiest of jobs, it was enough that I collapsed onto my bed and tried to sleep.

Chess had said he'd only be gone a few days at most, and not to worry, but of course telling me not to worry only made me worry more. So after tossing and turning for about an hour, my senses acutely aware of the hole, I gave up trying to get to sleep.

I made my way to the kitchen, and without turning on the kitchen light, opened the fridge door. The light from the door illuminated the contents of the kitchen and a quiet Alice sitting at the table. My heart leapt into my chest.

"What are you doing sitting in the dark?" I flipped on the kitchen light before turning back to her.

"Thinking." The one word said volumes to what she was thinking about. It was the same thing I had been thinking about since Chess left. The possibility that our worlds, the human and the Fae world, would go to war.

I wanted to believe that the human race was more open minded than that, but with the way we treated our own species, I had little hope that we wouldn't have the strike first and dissect later mentality. It didn't bode well for any Fae or half-breed.

"I don't know what to say to make you feel better, Alice." I opened the freezer and pulled out an ice cream carton. I grabbed two spoons from the drawer and sat down at the table. "Whatever will happen, will happen, but until that time comes, there is nothing that rocky road ice cream can't fix."

"Rocky road?" She cocked her head at the outstretched spoon and the carton in my hand. She took the spoon from me and watched as I peeled the top off the carton to reveal the decadent chocolate, almond, and marshmallow goodness inside.

Digging my spoon in, I took a big bite and simply moaned in delight. Literally, nothing could beat good old ice cream therapy. Okay, maybe a toe curling orgasm or two, but not much else.

Alice dipped the spoon into the carton, pulling out a small amount, and slipping it into her mouth. Her eyes lit up.

"Oh, my! That is good." She placed her hand to her mouth and then dug her spoon in again to get more.

"I told you." I gave a smug smile as I loaded my spoon with another bite.

She shoveled another spoonful into her mouth, no longer caring if she was ladylike or not. "This is the best thing I've ever tasted. How do you not simply spend all day eating these kinds of foods?"

"Well, for one, I would get really fat. Then there is diabetes, heart disease," I began, "But it's good for anxiety in a pinch and has been known to heal a broken heart in no time flat."

She cocked her head to the side. "But if you could eat this and feel so wonderful, why deal with men at all? I know it has been a while, but from the few times I have had relations, while they weren't altogether unpleasant, if you do not wish for a child, I do not see the point."

I laughed so hard I snorted. "Relations? You mean sex?"

"Yes, if you must be so crude." She blushed at the word.

"Sex is not crude by society's standards. *Fucking* would be crude." I laughed at the shocked expression on her face. "And if all you can say about your experiences was that they weren't unpleasant, your partner wasn't doing it right."

"I do not understand. How do you not do it right?" Her lip pushed out in a cute confused pout. "I did exactly as my mother instructed when she advised me in preparation to be married. I'll admit, the first time did hurt quite a bit, but after that, it wasn't so bad." She shrugged. "But I have to say, I do not understand what the whole fuss is about."

I paused, my spoon in midair, and then waved it at her. "There is a lot to fuss about. If you've only ever had all right sex, you'll never know what you are missing. And having bad sex can make or break any relationship."

"Much has changed since I was in this world. I fear I will never catch up." She shook her head and scooped another spoonful of icy goodness.

"Oh, Alice. There is so much to tell you. So much to teach you. I don't even know where to start." I stopped at that and giggled as I had a naughty thought. "Speaking of not needing men. Let me tell you about this wonderful invention called a vibrator."

CHAPTER

MIRROR, MIRROR

IT HAD BEEN several days since Alice and I gorged ourselves on ice cream. Things were beginning to get back to normal. With no new attacks, and no Fae showing up at my doorstep, I felt safe enough to go back to work.

So, while I was slaving away at work, Alice hung out, reacquainting herself with the human world, via reality TV.

"I still don't understand these silly women. How do they not know who the father of their children is?" Alice asked me the moment I stepped in the door.

She had taken to wearing my clothes instead of her usual tea dress and was lounging about on the couch in a pair of yoga pants that I knew said 'Bite me' on the butt and an oversized t-shirt. I had offered her one of my tank tops, but she had looked at me with such horror that I hadn't offered it again. I would think being around the Fae would make her less of a prude, but apparently, you could give a girl magical powers, but the thought of showing her shoulders was unspeakable.

"I told you to stop watching that crap." I plopped down on the couch next to her, glaring in disgust at the latest reality talk show she had taken up.

"But they are so interesting. How am I going to learn about this new world if I don't watch your magic box?" She gestured toward the TV, before grabbing a handful of chips from the bag on the coffee table.

"It's not magic." I snatched the bag from her and snagged my own pile of greasy goodness. "It's science. Electricity, wires, and such."

"All the same to me." Alice shrugged her shoulders. The neckline of her shirt fell off, which she yanked back up with a slight blush on her face.

In the last few days, I had taught her about the things she had missed, such as electricity and the Internet.

"Anyway, to answer your question, she doesn't know because she is a ho," I said through a mouthful of chips. Nothing like junk food to relieve the stress of a hard day at work.

"And being a garden tool is a bad thing?" Her brow furrowed in confusion.

I gave an impatient sigh. "A ho, as in a loose woman." I ignored the shocked gasp and continued, "As in someone who has sexual relations with multiple partners without taking the proper precautions."

"Right," she said slowly, though I wasn't sure she actually understood. "Well, this man is definitely the father, they have the same facial structure and everything."

"Yeah, well, sometimes people only see what they want to see." I stood from the couch and stretched. "On that note, I'm going to take a bath, holler if you need me."

"Lady?"

I paused at her voice.

"Have you heard anything or seen any...?"

She trailed off, but I knew what she meant. Had I seen any other Fae in this world? Thankfully, I hadn't. My day had been unremarkably boring. The only thing that worried me was the lack of a certain feline presence.

I hadn't seen or heard from Chess since he had left abruptly in the middle of the night. Every time I thought of that time, a smile crept up on my face, and over the last few days, it had happened more often than I'd like to admit.

"No, I haven't." The unspoken *yet* hung in the air.

I made my way to my bedroom for fresh clothing. A nagging worry pressed down on me. Where was he? He had said he needed to make preparations, but what kind of preparations could he make? There were many things I still didn't know, but I thought he was done keeping secrets. Apparently not.

We didn't know how the humans would react to the Fae, or if there was even anything to worry about. I'd been watching the news like crazy, and there hadn't been any state of emergency about unknown creatures as of yet. No doubt if there had been any word, my mother would have been all over my ass to move closer to town, or god forbid, in with her.

I shuddered at the thought as I snatched up my favorite pair of pajamas: a pair of red men's pajama pants and a black t-shirt that said, 'I'm here. What are your other two wishes?' I had found it hilarious at the time, but now knowing how wishing could end with your death, it wasn't that funny.

As I rummaged around for a clean pair of underwear, I had a vague feeling of being watched. I spun around. My eyes scanned the room. There was no one there. I had felt it. I was sure of it. But I almost shrugged it off when there was a movement. It was small, but there, behind the sheet thrown over my mirror was a figure.

I doubted they could see much into my room, but it didn't make me any less upset about it. Sitting my clothes down, I crept over to the mirror. Snatching up a hammer I had left out after patching up the hole, I held up my other hand to pull back the sheet. I yanked it back.

My mother, Queen of the Seelie Court, stood in the frame, an amused look on her face.

"What did you think you were going to do, human? Beat me to death?" She threw back her head and laughed, the sound of it grated on my nerves.

Standing there in all her splendor, she looked very much the queen she was. A white gown coated her figure, billowing out from mid-thigh and down to the floor. Her white blonde hair was piled up on her head in an extricated hairdo that I would have destroyed in five minutes.

"What are you doing here?" I asked, not beating around the bush. If she was here, it was because she wanted something. I would rather get it out of the way than stand there for hours listening to her pretend to care.

Her ice blue eyes narrowed, and I might have worried, but I was tired and really had no fucks left to give.

"Do not speak to me in such a way, human. I wish to speak to my daughter, bring her to me," she demanded as if it were so simple.

I shook my head. "It doesn't work that way, I'm afraid."

"Do you dare defy me?" She took a step back from the mirror as if appalled that anyone would even think it. The movement allowed me to see the white and gold of the throne room behind her. There was the distinct sound of chatter in the background, letting me know she was not alone.

Resisting the urge to return with a smartass remark, I took a seat on the edge of the bed. I was going to be here a while. Her usually cool and collected face morphed into rage.

"How dare you sit in the presence of your queen? Do you have a death wish, child?" She crossed her arms over her chest, tapping her nails against her arm.

"Mother," I stated in a firm and confident tone. "Please shut up."

"How dare you—"

"Stop," I snapped, my patience wearing out. "You do not come to my home and demand things of me. I am not the human, and I am not a child. I am the Seelie Princess that was once your daughter but now happens to reside in this human form. Regardless of our relations, you are not in any way my queen."

I could tell my words were just adding to the flame of her rage, but when she opened her mouth to speak, I cut her off again.

"As I see it, you need me." I waited for her to deny it, and when she didn't, I continued, "And while you may keep all the secrets you like from me, the truth of the matter is, you aren't in any position to demand anything of me."

"Well, see here now. There are things that must be done, rules that must be obeyed." For the first time in all my life, I saw fear in her eyes. "Events have already gone far beyond what we believed possible, and much of that I believe is your fault, not that silly little twit everyone else seems to blame."

"You're right." I stood from my seat and approached the mirror. "It's not her fault, and while some of the blame certainly falls on my shoulders, the base of the blame is all yours, Mother."

Her eyes widened, and her gaze darted around the room as if she realized an audience wasn't such a good idea for this conversation. Turning from the mirror, she muttered to a gold-plated guard. He began clearing the room.

"Not him." She pointed off to the side, and then returned her attention to me, with a suspicious, but worried expression. "What have you heard?"

"Not much, really." I shrugged.

It was true; I didn't know a whole lot, most of it was just conjecture I had gotten from the various misleading conversations with the citizens of the Underground. Then there were the visions I'd had with Seer.

Not to mention, the argument I had witnessed between my mother and Mab over what to do about the Shadows and then the tree, the tree that seemed to know everything but gave away so little. I'd give anything for an hour or two with that tree.

My mother waited for me to fill in the blanks. I didn't want to show her my whole hand, but unless I gave her something, she wasn't going to move an inch. There wasn't any time for there to be a stalemate between us.

"You and the UnSeelie Queen had a disagreement over what to do about the ones who are now known as the Shadows." I paused, and she nodded. "You didn't want to kill any more of our kind, and so you cast them out into the abyss that is now known as the Shadow Realm. What was it before?"

She hesitated, before indulging me, "A graveyard. What some refer to as the Reaper's playground."

"But how did you even get into there? I don't remember ever seeing anything in my studies about anyone even being able to reach it. It's not connected to the rest of the realms."

"Not directly, no." She pressed her lips together into a fine line as if it pained her to tell me anything about the door. "It took quite a bit of magic and some incantations to make a hole."

"The door in the Between with the rest?" I thought back to the beaten up door set in the circle with the others and the two-headed sisters that guarded them.

"Yes," she snapped, and then composed herself. "But now it's done, and if I could take it back I would, but the fact of the matter is that they are out now and looking for blood. Fae blood."

"I know. I was there." My voice was small and a bit ashamed of what I had done.

"So I've been told." Her anger fluttered in the air even through the glass.

Changing the subject off of my failings, I held my hands out. "So, what do I have to do to fix it?"

"It is quite simple." Her face began to light up.

"Well, if it is that simple, why does it have to be me?" I retorted. "Couldn't it be any half-blood?"

"No. It cannot." Her voice was blades on my skin. "It has to be you."

"Why?"

"As much as I loathe to admit it, you are the only one powerful enough to defeat them." She looked off to the side, bitterness on her face.

Was my being more powerful than her such a big deal? Knowing my mother, it was a very big deal. Having a weakling for a daughter was something she could handle but one more powerful than her? I was lucky she needed me, or I would have been dead already.

"Fine. What's the deal? A talisman I have to wave at them at the light of the moon? A sword made by Tibetan blind monks?" I said, naming off a few options I had seen in movies and books.

"Nothing of the sort. A little blood, a few words, and poof. Problem gone. The Shadows no more." A secret smile curled up her face, telling me she was holding back something.

"All right. Then we should just get it over with then, shouldn't we? Where are the Shadows at now?" I was suddenly glad I hadn't gotten ready for bed already and still had some decent clothes on. Not really fighting material, but it would work for this.

"Not so fast." She held her hands up. "The ritual itself is simple, of course, but from what I have learned, you are far from ready to face the Shadows."

"Not ready?" I frowned, wondering who had been speaking to her on my behalf. "I admit, I haven't quite mastered all of my powers in my human body, but I'm sure I could figure it out should it come down to it."

"It has nothing to do with your powers, but with you." She once again looked off to the side at something I couldn't see. I could hear some distant noise that could have been a groan or something else I equally didn't want to know about.

241

Ignoring the sound, I tried to get some answers. "What does it have to do with me?"

"How is your fiancé doing?" She turned her attention back to me, a small, mischievous smile on her face. The question came so far out of left field that I almost thought I'd misheard her.

What did Dorian have to do with any of this?

I frowned. "How should I know?"

"That's not what I heard." Her eyes locked with mine as if she knew more than she was saying and in her case, it was probably true. "I heard you stomped all over the poor Prince's heart after he caught you with our darling Jewels."

I gaped at her and then ground my teeth. Bastian the bastard had been spinning tales again. Next time I saw him, I was going to do more than kick him in the balls—I'd make a necklace out of them.

"Not that I blame you," she continued as if my expression didn't matter. "He is quite a delectable piece of meat, if a little full of himself."

"More like tried to mind rape me," I growled out, not believing my mother could ever find anyone but my father attractive.

"Nonsense." She waved her hand at me, dismissing my accusation. "He was only trying to fulfill his orders. You can hardly blame him for being a little over enthusiastic."

"Over enthusiastic?" I scoffed. "He tried to own me! If I wasn't as powerful as everyone says I am, I'd be his little sex slave right now, and that doesn't bother you?"

"I had no doubt you would have overcome any who would seek to control you, which is another topic I wanted to discuss." Her gaze turned serious as if she hadn't just tried to justify rape. "There may have been a few rumors about you that have gotten out into the populace. While I have heavy guards on the doors out of our world, you will want to be on the lookout."

"You are a little late on that. I had a nasty visit from a few faeries and a troll already." I crossed my arms, still irritated at the hole in my bedroom that was barely held together by a piece of plywood. "And what kind of rumors?"

All kinds of things began to run through my head. Anything could be going around. From my involvement with the Shadows to my crazy powers. Either way, it was best to know what I was to be prepared for.

"A troll? Really? How did you ever get away from it in that pathetic human body?" She laughed, not making me feel any better.

"What kind of rumors, Mother?" I ground out, choosing to be the bigger person and ignore her blatant insults.

"Very well, if you must know." She sniffed. "Someone, I do not know who, let on that your blood has some kind of magical properties, and that they could gain your powers by draining you."

"What?" My voice rose to a high-pitched squeak. "That's ridiculous, you cannot transfer powers between Fae, not even through blood."

My mother shrugged. "I did not say it was a logical rumor, only that some of the people have begun to believe it, and they could very well attack you."

It made sense now why the faeries had attacked. They had tasted my blood before, and no doubt it was easy to sway them into believing the rumor was true. If they believed it to be true, it would be too easy to convince some of the other Faes to believe it, as well. As if my life was not complicated enough as it was.

"Fine. Consider me warned. Now, what do I have to do to be ready?" I tried to steer the conversation back to the larger threat.

"You will know when you are." She turned, as if to end the conversation, but stopped mid-turn. "Oh yes, one more thing. I found something of yours."

"What?" I asked. I didn't remember losing anything.

"He was found snooping around, and since he had been avoiding me for a while now, we had a lot of catching up to do." I suddenly knew who she had been looking at through our conversation.

"What did you do?" I snarled, my anger flaring to life.

The power in me crackled along my skin. The grunting from before had to have come from Chess. With all the horrible things she had already forced on him, I couldn't imagine the horrors of what he had been subjected to now.

"Do not get upset." She tutted at me as if chastising a child. "He was mine before he was ever yours, and I was simply trying to get what was owed to me." She frowned off to the side, irritation filling her face. "But I see that I will not be getting my full payment anytime soon, so you may have him back."

She waved her hand to a guard, and the sound of something being dragged drew my attention to the side of the mirror. My eyes landed on an unconscious Chess, beaten and bloodied.

The guards left him lying in a crumbled pile in front of the mirror. He had to be touching the mirror for it to work, but he wasn't awake to do anything of the sort. I stared at my mother. She sat on her throne watching in amusement at my distress.

Narrowing my eyes in determination, I knew what I had to do. Having only activated a mirror once before and only in the Underground, I wasn't entirely sure it would work, but I reached my hand out, anyway. I touched my hand to the frame of the mirror and poured my powers into it. At first, nothing happened. Then the solid glass began to ripple. I placed my hand on cool liquid, the feel of it swirling around my skin still foreign to me. Bending down, I stuck both arms through the surface and grabbed a hold of Chess.

He was heavier than he looked. I grunted at the effort it took to move him even an inch, while my mother watched me with amusement. Growling, I placed one foot on each side of the mirror and yanked Chess through the mirror's surface.

When he was back on my side and safe in my arms, I glared back at the mirror. It had become solid again, and the smirking face of my mother was fading from view.

This wasn't over. Not by a long shot.

CHAPTER

BROKEN BUT STILL FABULOUS

I HELD CHESS against me to take in the damage to his body. Bruises marred his beautiful face, making his eyes puffy and swollen; his usual grinning lips were split. The pale pink of his locks was colored dark brown where blood had dried in his hair and his garments were in shambles. I could see where a blade had torn into him through the rips in his clothes. I needed to take care of him, fast.

"Alice!" I yelled. "Help!"

As I was checking to see if he was still bleeding, Alice rushed in.

"My goodness!" She gasped.

"Don't you faint on me," I warned as I tried to lift him up, but found myself lacking super strength. What was the point of improved senses if I didn't get the whole shebang?

"I would never." She scoffed and knelt beside me.

Being careful not to bump him, I twisted around to see how far the bed was away from us. It wasn't that far, maybe a couple of feet; two small girls like us could handle it. Probably.

"Just help me get him onto the bed." My voice strained as I tried to lift him into my arms.

Alice tried to pick him up around his waist.

"No, don't," I snapped. "Grab his legs. There're fewer injuries there. We don't want to damage him any more than he already is."

It took us three tries before we finally dragged him onto the bed. It wasn't the most graceful or efficient way to do it, but we got it done. Squatting down to unlace his boots that were miraculously still intact, I motioned to Alice.

"Go into the bathroom and get me some clean towels," I grunted as I tried to get the boot off of his muscular calf. "Then get under the sink and grab the box that has a cross on it that says first aid."

"Understood." Alice made for the door while I wrestled with his other boot.

Once both feet were free and, thankfully uninjured, I returned to his chest, where his skin peeked through the cuts in his clothes. Just seeing him like this made my blood boil.

The cuts were the same as before. The old scars on his body I had tried to ask him about time and time again, had they also been from my mother? It only made sense that they would have come from her as well.

"Grab some water from the kitchen!" I called.

Alice hollered back an *okay* from the bathroom.

"Now, let's get these pants off of you," I mumbled to myself, while my face heated up at the thought of seeing him nude for the first time.

I had imagined seeing him naked plenty of times. Most of them in my dreams. But in every scenario, I had never imagined the first time I got his pants off would be like this.

"Here you are." Alice brought in the items I had requested and sat them on the edge of the bed. She arched her brow as I stood with my hands at the waist of his

249

pants, but not moving. "What are you doing?"

"Should I wake him?" I let go of his pants and stepped back. "I should wake him, shouldn't I? I mean, I wouldn't want to be disrobed without my knowledge."

"But wouldn't it be easier to clean his wounds while he is unconscious?" Alice reasoned. "Besides, I don't think he would care, either way. I think this is more of you having an issue with seeing him disrobed. But you know, if you'd rather not, I could always—"

"No!" I cut in, before adding, "I mean no, and it's all right. It's just me being silly. I got this. You can go back to your reality shows. I'll call if I need anything."

I waved her off, suddenly more than ready to get on with it.

She gave me a knowing grin before shuffling out the door.

"It's okay." I shook the nerves out of my hands, trying to pep myself up for what I had to do. "You can do this. Just think of it like you are taking care of a relative. Not a hunky Fae, who may or may not be your boyfriend."

The last bit didn't make me feel any better.

With a deep breath, I quickly unbuttoned his pants and pulled down the zipper. My eyes grew large, and my gaze darted up to the ceiling when I realized Chess liked to go all-natural underneath his pants. It really shouldn't have surprised me.

With my eyes on the ceiling, I got the pants off his butt, but maneuvering them down his legs became a problem. Throwing a towel over his fun bits, I tried my best to not be too interested in them as I surveyed his wounds.

The pants stuck to him from where the blood had dried on his legs. Grabbing the scissors from the first aid kit, I cut around the wounds and peeled the pants away.

He groaned and began to mutter words that I couldn't make out. I leaned in, hoping to catch some of what he was saying.

"Hearts," he mumbled, and I waited for him to continue. He remained silent.

"What about the hearts?" I urged.

"Not ready. Won't give her the hearts," he answered, his lips flopping over themselves from the puffiness.

"What hearts?"

He didn't speak further.

"Well, that was entirely unhelpful." I waited to see if he would wake up and stifled a giggle when he snorted.

He didn't seem to be waking up, though.

God that would have been embarrassing. I could imagine the look on his face, not to mention what he'd have to say if he saw me at his waist trying to rip his pants off. I couldn't keep the heat from filling my face as I got the rest of his clothes off.

When he was completely nude, sans the towel over his bits, I tried to take in the damage. Most of the bleeding had stopped, and there weren't any internal organs spilling out of him, thank God. Blood I could deal with, but organs not so much. Luckily, none of the cuts were very deep. They seemed more for torture rather than to actually cause him mortal injury.

"What did she want from you?" I asked myself as I set to work on cleaning him up.

It didn't take long for the water Alice brought me to turn pink, but I was able to clean most of him up before it needed to be changed. Since nothing needed stitches from what I could tell—not that I knew how to do that, or could really take him to a doctor for that matter—I simply covered them with bandages. Unfortunately, my bandaging skills were lacking, leaving most of his torso looking like a mummy.

By the time I had him cleaned up and bandaged, it was well past my bedtime. Too exhausted to care about being in bed with the lecherous feline, I crawled onto the other side of the mattress and collapsed onto my pillow. I turned on my side to watch him as my eyes began to droop, and then I was gone.

* * *

I WOKE TO the sound of a male voice groaning and the bed shifting next to me. I bolted upright when I realized what was happening. Chess had sat up on the bed and was in the process of trying to get up.

I put my hands on his arm. "Lay back down. You shouldn't be moving around so much."

He hesitated, and then complied with my wishes, though it was probably more because of the pain than anything.

"What happened?" He watched me beneath his pale eyelashes with a pained look on his face.

"You tell me?" I lay back down next to him, my gaze focused on his face and not the way the sheet had dipped at his waist.

His eyes went up to the ceiling, and he was quiet for a long time. So long that I thought he wasn't going to answer.

"I went to tell your mother to leave you alone," he said, at last, his voice was soft.

I thought I saw a faint blush on his face.

"But I thought you went to make preparations in case other Fae got out?" It was admirable that he would put himself in danger for my sake, and he obviously didn't do that sort of thing often.

"I did—make preparations that is. When I was finished, I confronted the queen." He said the word queen like it was a vile word, which I was beginning to think it was as well. No queen would do what my mother had done and have a clear conscious. I know I couldn't have.

"Why would you do that? It's not like she could really do anything to me. I mean, she needs me, right?" I frowned.

"And that is why, my pet, she must leave you alone." He looked me dead in the eyes, seriousness in his tone. "Let her find another way to get rid of the Shadows."

His eyes gave away more than he was saying. Something was wrong. What did he know about defeating the Shadows that my mother hadn't already told me?

"Why? It's just a little blood and some words. She told me herself." Even if she had been lying, it wasn't like I could tell through a mirror. But I doubt she would have lied

254

right to my face in front of those in the room with her. Even if it was only the guards.

"Yes, I suppose that is all it is." Chess barked out a laugh, and then grabbed his side and moaned.

"Then what?" I sat up from the bed. "What's the big deal?"

"The big deal?" His eyes filled with anger. Whether it was anger at me or anger at my mother, I didn't know. "The big deal, little girl, is your mother, Queen of the Fucking Underground, is offering up her own daughter for slaughter." He gave a dark laugh again. "And just after the kingdom thinks we got you back."

I didn't understand. I heard the words he was saying, but they didn't make any sense. How could I be going to my death? Nothing anyone had said had portrayed me dying, and a little blood certainly didn't bring thoughts of death to mind.

"Hey." He turned his emerald eyes to me, the anger in them gone. He reached out with one clawed hand and cupped my face. "Do not worry, love. You won't die if I have anything to say about it."

"Because I'm not ready, right?" I tried not to let my uncertainty at his words show.

Something passed behind his eyes, but he simply smiled. "Right, so..." He trailed off, looking down at the sheet covering him. "You couldn't wait until I was conscious to tear my clothes off?"

"You wish. Alice did it," I lied, letting him change the topic, because it was getting depressing, even for me.

His eyes lit up in surprise, but he leaned in close to me until his nose was a hair from my neck. "I don't think she did, did she?"

My breathing became shallow. I swallowed and stuttered out, "Yes, she did. I faint at the sight of blood."

Chess loomed above me, the sheet all but gone. My body stiffened. I kept my eyes on him as he lowered himself to his elbows, allowing his lower half to press against me. If I hadn't already been breathless, that would have done it for me.

"You forget, my kitty Kat." He took a big inhale of my scent and growled. "I can smell you, and you smell like a lie."

Instead of answering, I focused on the bandages that were now colored red. "You're bleeding, you know."

"Damn." He rolled off me with a wince. "You sure know how to kill the mood, love."

I gave a nervous chuckle. "That's me, mood killer and virgin sacrifice."

"Virgin?" Chess quirked his brow.

"Okay, not virgin, but you know what I mean." My face had to have been as red as a tomato right then. I got off the bed to get more bandages as a diversion.

"You stayed with me?" He questioned as I dug through the box of supplies. "Why?"

"Because I care about you. Why else?"

"No one has ever cared about me. Not enough to stay by my side through the night." He said it so softly I almost didn't hear him.

"Someone must have cared for you." I turned from the box, an aching beginning in my heart. "Your mother? Father?"

"No. No one." He shook his head, his dirty hair hanging around his face, hiding the darkness that had overcome his features. "I didn't get to know my mother. She bore me as was her duty and then gave me to my father who tolerated a half Seelie child who was like him but not in so many ways. He was strict, and yet had a way of knowing exactly what everyone needed, but never me."

"I'm sure he cared." I approached the bed, my words more meaning to comfort

257

myself than him. "He must have, maybe he just didn't know how to show it."

"Perhaps." His voice was small, as if he couldn't begin to believe it.

"What happened to him?"

"Oh, well, after the queen found out I couldn't give her what she wanted, she paid my father for the right to have me be the moderator. I haven't seen him since." He kept his eyes down while I went about changing his bandages. The cuts were starting to heal already, thank God for Fae abilities.

"That's terrible. How old were you?" I tried to keep the conversation going, no matter how upsetting, to either distract him, or me I wasn't sure which.

"Thirteen."

"So young?" I had a horrible, disgusting thought. "Wait. They didn't pay you the same way they do now, did they?"

"Oh, no." Chess laughed at the horror on my face. "I didn't start getting paid until I was of age and could become of some use to her. I was given a home and food, but I had to find my own friends and make my own fun."

"That must have been very lonely." I felt my heart break a little for him. I might be a loner by nature, but not to have anyone there, not even a parent, was unimaginable.

"Well, it was a long time ago, and I have plenty of friends now, and I have..." He trailed off, looking down at me with uncertainty.

"Me," I filled in for him. "You have me."

"Yes. I do, don't I?" He gave me a smile that made my heart feel like it would burst from my chest.

So instead of dealing with the sudden influx of emotion, I did what anyone would have done: fled.

"I'm going to go check on Alice." I stood abruptly, ignoring the startled look on his face as I closed the door behind me.

As I made my way to the living room, I tried to still the thundering in my chest. I remembered this emotion. It was something I'd promised myself I'd never feel again after what happened with Dorian. I couldn't feel this way. Not already.

It was barely dawn, and Alice was already on the couch, watching some early morning talk show.

"How is he?" She glanced up from the TV briefly.

"He's awake and getting better, but he said something I wanted to confirm with you," I explained to her how Chess was born and what he had to deal with on his own. When I finished, I had to ask, "Did you know about this?"

"About Chess? Yes, unfortunately, I did. I told you I have talked to him before. He had come to my mirror a few times, each time wanting to know why I did this to him." She shrugged, as if there was nothing new about it and to her it probably wasn't.

"You? How was it your fault?"

"Why does anyone think it is my fault?" She scoffed, turning back to her show and the never-ending bag of chips she kept finding.

Where was she getting them? I swore I never kept junk food in the house, besides my ice cream fix, because I had no self-control when it came to food. I'd be as big as a house if I didn't keep them out of the cupboards.

I did know why anyone would think it was her fault, though. She seemed to be the go-to person for the blame whenever something went wrong. Just because of one stupid wish.

"Sometimes, I wish I had never made that silly wish and had just stayed here. Then none of this would have happened. You would be happy with your prince, and the Shadows would not even be a problem."

260

Her blue eyes glanced longingly around the room as if the cheap wallpaper with dancing flowers was a palace.

"The Shadows would still have been a problem that needed to be dealt with," I assured, sitting next to her on the couch.

As I sat beside her recalling my conversation with Chess, I realized something. This started before I became human. Before the tree and my wish. Even before Dorian and I got engaged.

Could my mother really be that evil? She surely wasn't capable of such depravity. But all the answers, the half-breeds, the need for a half-breed to defeat the shadows, all of it seemed to focus entirely on me. It had always been me.

Jumping up from the couch, I eyed the curious Alice. "Keep an eye on him, will you?"

"Where are you going?" She didn't move from her spot on the couch. I think I'd created a monster. Shaking my head, I started for the kitchen door.

"What do I tell Chess if he asks?" She finally looked up from her show.

"Just tell him I'll be back and not to worry." I glanced toward the bedroom, anxiety filling me. I didn't want to leave him in his vulnerable state, but I needed to know.

"But where are you going?" Alice stood up now, confusion crinkling her face.

"It's time for me to go home."

CHAPTER

20

QUEEN OF THE UNDERGROUND

THIS TIME, WHEN I entered the cave at the pond behind the house and saw the glowing swirling glyphs, I didn't stop to ooh and ahh at them. Instead, I marched to the back of the cave where the opening was. When I stood in front of the hole, I didn't think about the bugs that could be living in there, or the time in that movie someone's arm got bit off. I simply shoved my hand in the hole and prepared myself for the straw slurping feeling.

Too soon, I was thrown out of the portal, through the open door, and straight on the floor. I held my hands out to brace for the impact. It didn't hurt as much this time around since I knew what was coming, but it still smarted like no other. I pulled myself up and was stunned by the sight before me.

The reception desk was in shambles. The monitor where Type, one of the two heads of the bird sisters, liked to watch Game of Thrones was smashed to pieces. The glass still littered the pure white floor. The wood of the desk was splintered, and pieces of it were scattered all around the white void. The desk was nothing compared to the doors.

The doors that led to the Seelie and UnSeelie Realms had been blown off their hinges. Even the door I had come through was no longer in its place. It too lay shattered on the ground. In place of the doors, to my relief, were guards of the Seelie Court. Each door had their own set of guards except the one I had come through, and the only door that was still intact: the door to the Shadow Realm.

I could only think that the door was the hole my mother had talked about opening. Why would she put it here? Where anyone could get to it? Maybe she was just lazy and made it easier on herself to find. Like before, there was no handle to the worn and burn marked door, and if anything, it looked even more beat up. It was as if someone from the inside was trying to get out.

There were two guards covered in gold plated armor in front of the two doors to the Fae courts. As if two apiece would stop any intruders that were determined to leave. Or enter, in my case.

The guards watched me with cautious eyes, not moving from their posts. Last time I had gone through the UnSeelie door, since that was where Trip and Mop were from, but this time, I headed for the door to the Seelie Court. I could only hope it would be faster than finding my way to Chess' house again.

Stopping in front of the guards, I took them in. They were both equally attractive, as most of the Seelie Court Fae were. Knowing my mother though, they were guards because they weren't beautiful by Fae standards, but in the human realm, they would have still gotten hit on by any woman in their right mind. One had dark hair that hung to his shoulders and bronze colored skin, while the other had almost pitch-black skin and in a striking contrast, white hair.

"Let me pass," I addressed them both, digging down to bring out my inner princess to push a commanding tone out that they would obey.

The guards looked between themselves, their faces equally conflicted. One of them even leaned out from his post to glance at the two guards in front of the other door. Those two shook their head at them in response.

"You shouldn't be here right now, your highness. It isn't safe." The guard with bronze coloring tried to appease me with reason.

"I wish to see my mother, the queen, and I demand you move aside." I kept my voice even but firm, allowing it alone to pave my way.

The two looked at each other again, a hint of fear in their eyes. Were they afraid of me? Or my mother?

"But we have strict orders that none may pass through these doors, or it's our heads. Not after the faeries and that half-breed got through," the guard with the hair that almost blended into the room around us bit out a gruff reply.

"Don't forget the troll," One of the guards from the other door finally spoke up. Apparently, my mother was the scarier of the two. I would have to fix that and soon.

My guard nodded. "Right, and the troll."

"Don't worry, I will take full responsibility, but it is urgent I see my mother." Since diplomacy wasn't working, I tried for being their friend.

"I'm sorry, really I am, but I have kids. I can't get stuck in a mirror cell." The bronze god shook his head in apology and turned his eyes away as if to dismiss me.

I crossed my arms over my chest, irritation flittering through me. How was I going to get in to see her if they wouldn't let me in? I could go back and just use the mirror in my room, but then I'd have to deal with explaining what I was doing to Chess, and I wasn't ready to see him again yet. I could try to rush them, but they were at least 200 pounds each, and I was pushing 140, barely. Or I could use my new powers to throw them out of the way.

I was getting ready to do just that when a voice called out, "Let her pass."

The guards parted to reveal Seer as she stepped into the doorway of the Seelie Court in all her blue glory. Her pixie cut, periwinkle blue hair was swept up into a fauxhawk, giving her more of a 'don't fuck with me' attitude that was only insinuated more by her floor length electric blue body suit. I bet it was a bitch to get that skintight suit on over her wings, but with six arms, she had the advantage. Those said arms were crossed over her chest as her obsidian eyes narrowed in on the guards, daring them to challenge her.

"Seer." The guards bowed their heads as they moved out of her way.

Seer ignored them and came over to me, her arms, all six of them, stretched out to envelop me in a warm, yet awkward, hug. I stood as stiff as a board and let her get her greeting out before gently untangling myself from her arms. Like Chess, she could get a little out of hand if I didn't put down boundaries. Not like that had ever stopped the cat.

"While I'm happy to see you, what are you doing in the Seelie Court?" In the past, it hadn't been an everyday occurrence where a Fae left their respective court. From what Mop had told me, it was even more unlikely now.

"You are not the only one worried in this troubled time." Giving me a small smile, she wrapped a couple of arms around me and pulled me to her side. She turned to the guards who resumed their posts in front of the door. "The human is not only your princess, but our savior. Would you dare deny her passage?" She eyed the two guards, who stood speechless. Seer turned to all of the guards. "Remember, she will be the one who destroys the Shadows and save us. She'll save us all."

Her words were too close to those of the mysterious tree. I shot her a curious look, and she smiled that knowing smile I was beginning to hate. As much as I wanted to question her, it wasn't the time. Questions later. I had more pressing matters to attend to.

Seer escorted me through the doorway and past the unhappy guards. Unlike when I had entered the Underground the first time, I stepped out onto a marble floor, instead of face down on the ground.

Walking down the gold-colored hallways, arm and arm with Seer, I bit my lip and asked, "Did you know about Chess?"

"I don't have to have the sight to know the cat's plight. Everyone knew." Seer frowned.

"How could you know what he was going through and do nothing?" I stopped in my tracks, pulling her around to look at me.

Seer turned to me with a weary smile. "It is not like we didn't try. Unlike those Seelie snots and, with the exception of your betrothed, we UnSeelie do not turn our backs on our kind, half-blood or not."

I opened my mouth to ask about my mother's intentions for me, but she beat me to it.

"Do not worry. Everything will come to pass the way it should, and something's are better to be forgiven and forgotten, rather than dwelling on them. Your mother did what she thought was best at the time, even if it meant losing you."

I frowned at her words. If she knew what I was there for, what I needed confirmation of, then I had no doubt in my mind that my mother had done exactly what I thought she had. I had always believed she had my happiness in mind, even when she was taking heads left and right in the name of justice. I thought one of those moments was when she introduced me to my betrothed, but even that act was tainted.

The anger I had felt when Chess told me about his childhood mixed with the confirmation from Seer made my magic whip around inside me like a hurricane. It forced me to storm past Seer and on to where I knew the throne room lie. Large double doors covered in intricate vines of gold and bronze lie between my mother and me. Without giving myself time to chicken out, I wrenched the doors open, the sound of them slamming against the wall echoed through the room.

Inside the throne room, which hadn't changed from its golden and white decoration, sat my mother and her court. The white columns of the room held up the golden ceiling and the nobles, while more clothed than last time, still matched the décor.

My father, to my unfortunate luck, was present. I didn't want his presence to lessen my anger. It was the only thing keeping me from shrinking back from the curious and somewhat contrite glances I was getting from the court.

"Daughter, what an unexpected surprise." My mother, ever the politician, sat on her throne. "What are you doing here?"

Not caring about the nobles lining the room, I marched up to stand before the throne. My eyes met my father's, who gave me a small smile in welcome. Though his face was young, his eyes showed his age and weariness of it all. By this time, he should have retired, and I should have ruled with my husband, but since I was the only heir and I had died, there was no one to take their place. It wasn't like my mother wanted to give up her power, anyway.

271

"I'm sure you know exactly what I'm here about." My rage crackled in my voice.

"The half-breed," my mother responded without hesitation, a small smirk spreading across her face.

"How could you do that to him? To any of them?" I chanced a glance at my father, and I could see the shame and regret cover his face. At least one of them showed remorse.

"I am doing what I think is best for our kingdom. If a few half-breeds get hurt along the way, who is going to care?"

The crowd of nobles chuckled, and she smiled at them.

"I do." My voice was clear as I laid down the line of where I stood in this fight.

"One among thousands." She giggled, the sound of it like nails on a chalkboard. She stood from her throne, her golden gown melting around her as she moved. "You would be their champion? You cannot belong to both worlds. Either you are part of ours, or theirs."

I held my ground as she moved to me. When I was Fae, I would have been able to meet her eyes with no problem, but in my human form I barely came up to her breasts. Which was probably why she was trying to use her height to intimidate me into submitting. My mother always was one to use what weapons were at hand.

"Then I would choose theirs every time." I stared straight up into her eyes, never flinching.

She watched my face as if she hadn't heard me correctly. Searching for something that I had been telling everyone wasn't there anymore. I wasn't the little princess who did what mommy told her. For once in my hundred and fifty years, I was standing on my own two feet, and no one was going to make me back down.

"What happened to you, Daughter? Does your human blood addle your mind?"

The nobles gave a nervous chuckle.

"Our world is about power, and when you ascend to the throne, you will be a great and mighty queen. Then, if you want to save all the half-breeds, you are free to do so, but until then, you will follow my rules and do as I say, or you might find yourself one or two kittens short of a litter."

"Answer me this one question, Mother," I implored, ignoring the fact that she had basically threatened Chess' life.

"Ask your question," she snapped, moving back toward her throne.

"Did you arrange my marriage so I would produce a half-breed heir for the sole purpose to use against the Shadows?" I let the question hang in the air as the room quieted. Every eye was on the Seelie Queen.

My mother gave an elegant shrug. "Of course I did. What do you think all these mutts are running around for?"

"Then yes, I have chosen a side."

"Good." My mother moved to sit back down on her throne, seemingly done with our conversation. "Then we will prepare for your move back to the palace."

She motioned to a servant that sped away to do just that.

"I meant, yes, I choose them. The half-breeds." I let it set in for a moment, before continuing, "I don't know what happened to you, Mother. When did you become so heartless? Or maybe you have always been that way and I have just now realized it. You say that we cannot afford to lose any more of our kind, and yet, you damn us with the choices you've made. And then here you are saying that those who are not pure are not worthy to be saved? You are no worse than the Fae you condemned to darkness," I snarled at her, my magic buzzing along my skin in agreement.

"How dare you speak to me that way! I am your queen." She stomped her foot like a child and snapped her fingers. "Guards!

Seize her. Daughter or not, you will do as you are told."

At her words, my senses became alert to the guards in the room. There was perhaps a half dozen. Not as many as there normally would have been, but I assumed most of them were off chasing the escaped Fae.

I waited to see what they would do, if they would really follow the orders of a mad queen. When they were close enough to surround me, I could see the uncertainty and unwillingness on their faces. They didn't agree with what their queen was doing. Whether it was putting me in a cell, or what was happening with the half-breeds, or a mixture of everything, my mother was losing her people, and now it was up to me.

"What are you waiting for?" My mother's voice called out sharp as ice along my skin, and the guards descended onto me like a stack of cards.

My magic was ready for them. It had been waiting for this very moment and was tired of being in control. It wanted to play. I released the built up energy. Just like cards, the guards blew away.

Unlike when I had fought the faeries, these guards didn't go down so easily. The moment they fell to the ground, they were back on their feet and coming for me.

I was not a fighter. I didn't know martial arts. I knew basic self-defense, enough to get away from one single attacker, but more than that? I was screwed.

My eyes darted around the room, trying to think of something to disable them. My eyes landed on a small tree near the double doors, and I remembered what happened at my mom's house. I made the plants grow from just my magic. It had been incredible. I had felt powerful and invincible, and while the thought of a power drain was not anything I wanted to happen again, I didn't have any other choice.

Not close enough to the plant to push my magic into it directly, I bent down on the marble floor and pressed my hands to the surface. My actions caused the guards to pause. Looking down at my hands, I could see why they would hesitate.

Green swirling energy spilled from my hands and made its way across the floor, searching and poking, looking for some kind of opening to pour themselves into.

"What are you fools doing?" My mother screamed from her throne. "Stop her!"

Shaking their heads, they drew their swords.

They inched toward me, their steps unsure and wary of the magic at their feet. Ignoring them, I pushed my magic to go to the planter, feeding into it, making it mine.

It didn't take long for the plant to respond. The small tree like foliage broke the glass around it, its roots spreading out across the floor. The green leaves grew to the size of footballs, and its limbs filled out swinging around it, trying to hit anyone who came near.

The nobles cried out and scattered. The guards turned their backs on me, their focus now on the growing monstrosity I had created.

Blood pumping in my ears, I forced more magic into it. My adrenaline spiked and an overwhelming need clouded my mind. It wasn't big enough, powerful enough. I needed more.

The small tree turned ginormous, sprouting vines that whipped out at the guards. They swung their swords trying to hack at it, but it was too strong. I was too strong.

As the vines wrapped around the guards, immobilizing them a feeling of triumph filled me. I didn't have long to celebrate before my head was yanked back, breaking my connection with my creation. My eyes searched out my mother's face and winced at the bite of her nails in my hair.

"Enough." She snarled in my ear, pulling on my hair.

"It will never be enough." I twisted in her grasp until I was facing her, my head at an odd angle. Smirking at the shock on her face, I placed my hands on her and forced my magic into her. I expected her to let go right away, but her magic fought against mine.

Like a razor, it sliced at my magic, but for each hole she made, more filled its place. Still, she held onto my hair like a lifeline.

Growling my impatience, I jerked my head in her hand before slamming my forehead into her nose. The brunt force sent a ringing in my ears that was overpowered by the relief of her hand dropping from my hair.

She clutched her face as blood dripped from her nose, staring at me. The fearless queen was no longer in control and she knew it.

I held my hand up and pushed my energy at her, shoving her back until she fell to the steps of her dais. Turning away from her sprawled form, I took in the surrounding room. The nobles inched back when my gaze landed on them and the guards lay unconscious on the ground leaving a path out of the throne room in their wake.

My eyes landed on the creature I had created. It sat there, still large but not attacking. Waiting.

Part of me celebrated in what I had created, while the other part was horrified. Did I keep it or put it back the way it was? I looked over the creature and saw the veins of my magic coming from it and had an idea.

Calling to the magic, I watched in awe as it slid out of the monster and slowly crept back under my skin. With each sliver of magic, I felt more powerful and more alive than before. The drain I had felt the first time I had used so much magic was nonexistent.

Not looking back on my still shouting mother, I took a step over one of the guards and toward the doors. I watched the nobles around me, waiting to see if they would be the next to attack. It was when I got to the door that I realized none of them would. While I might be a human, and a reluctant princess, in their eyes, I was now their queen.

Now if only I could earn it.

CHAPTER

21

CHESHIRE S. CAT

THE GUARDS IN the Between let me back out without hesitation, but with a hint of fear in their eyes. Word traveled fast in the Underground. Not that I was complaining.

Within moments, I was back in my kitchen.

"What happened?" Alice turned from the sink.

"It went as I expected." As I filled her in on the events that had occurred, and the realization that my mother had masterminded the whole situation for the specific reason of sacrificing my child, her own grandchild, to defeat the Shadows, a sense of weariness spread through me.

It had been a long night. Hell, a long century. And all I wanted was to take a long hot shower and go to sleep in my warm bed.

The bed that currently housed an injured feline.

"How is Chess doing?" I tilted my head toward the empty plate in her hand.

Alice pressed her lips together; displeasure and frustration clear on her face.

"I tried to be a kind hostess in your stead by bringing him something to eat, but what do I get for my troubles? Yelled at!" She placed the dish in the sink with more force than I would have liked. I only had so many dishes left after my own fit of destruction.

"Where is he now?" I sighed, running my hand through my hair.

"Still in bed. Says he was going to wait right there for you to return and wouldn't move an inch any sooner." She crossed her arms over her chest, looking the epitome of the snotty little girl she used to be.

"I better go check on him." I pointed my thumb toward the bedroom, backing out to end the conversation.

Down the hall, I opened the door to my bedroom and walked in, coming face-to-face with a much healed, and very nude Chess, standing in front of the bed.

I promptly flipped around.

"What are you doing up?" My voice squeaked as I stared hard at the bedroom door.

"Trying to salvage what little there is left of my pants." His voice was nonchalant, as if he wasn't standing there completely nude. "If you were so impatient to get me undressed you could have woken me, at least to save the pants."

My eyes fell on the pile of laundry I had yet to do sitting by the door. I grabbed the set of clothes I had intended to wear the previous night.

Without turning around, I called over my shoulder, "I'm going to shower."

I darted out the door and closed it on his answer, my mind already set on showering, and not on the image of his naked body burned into my retinas.

With the hot water pouring down me, I leaned my forehead against the wall. So much had happened over the last few weeks, it was hard to keep up. I'd moved back home, gotten a job I didn't really want, and then got sucked into another world, only to be spit back out as their princess.

Now, not only did my kingdom want me back, but also they wanted me to defeat an evil force that I already had a sort of kind of deal with. Not to forget that defeating the

Shadows could very well kill me. Even with all of my memories as the Fae Princess, it was still hard to believe it was all real.

I turned around and came face to face with a smirking Chess. Jumping in place with a squeal, my feet gave out from under me. I grabbed my grandmother's support bar on the wall and half caught myself from smashing face first into Chess' rather impressive parts.

Clutching the bar like a lifeline, I tried to angle my body away so I wasn't showing off all my goods to his searching eyes. "What the fuck do you think you are doing?"

Chuckling at my disgraceful scrambling on the shower floor, Chess reached up and turned the shower spray on him. "Like I tried to tell you before you ran away, while you did an excellent job patching me up, I still feel quite dirty."

"You could have waited until I was finished!" I climbed to my feet, keeping my back to his wet luscious body.

"In my fragile state? What if I had needed your help? I could have fallen and died in the shower. You wouldn't want that to happen, would you?" I could just hear the smiling in his voice. He was enjoying this far too much.

He reached around me to grab the loofa off the rack in front of me, and I gripped my arms over my chest, yipping like a little dog.

"Stay on your side!" I said, and then added, "And close your eyes."

"Very well." He sighed his reluctant agreement, but his tail whipped out and stroked along my inner thigh.

"And keep your tail to yourself!" I clamped my legs closed, pushing his appendage away.

"Will you clean my back?" He held the loofa out in front of my face.

"Do it yourself," I said between clenched teeth.

"But I can't reach it on my own, even with a tail." I could just imagine the pout on his face.

Giving in, I jerked the loofa from his grasp. "Fine, turn around, though, and no hanky-panky."

"Of course."

I peeked over my shoulder to be sure that he had indeed twisted around before lowering my arms from my chest and turning to him. With his eyes not on me, I could now look my share. I placed the loofa on his lean and muscular back, sliding it up and down to spread the soap along his skin. The water dripped down his back, displaying every ripple and curvature. My eyes followed the suds down the line of his spine to where his delicious butt stood high and taut where his tail hung toward the ground.

Though he was nude before me, my eyes were drawn to where the tail protruded out of his body. It wasn't like it was just attached like a piece of a costume, but like it was an extension of his spine. His tail always seemed to have a mind of its own, not always portraying the mood on his face. I must have been staring too long, because his voice startled me.

"You can touch it, if you want." His words were thick and deep as if my hand on his back had been enough to bring up his desire.

"Uh. All done." I gave a nervous chuckle and dropped the loofa before bolting from the shower.

I grabbed the thick robe on the back of the bathroom door and yanked open the door, not bothering to put it on before leaving.

With the robe firmly wrapped around me, I opened the bedroom door to find a wet and tempting Chess waiting for me.

"How do you keep doing that?" I turned my back on him, not ready to face the nude Fae full on.

"Half-breed, remember? The rules don't apply to us." His voice was filled with humor at my discomfort.

"But I can't go through walls." I attempted to keep the topic off of the elephant in the room. The very wet, very masculine, and yummy elephant that I wanted to climb onto and ride.

"You could if you wanted to." His voice was by my ear, and when his hands touched my shoulders, I couldn't help but tense up.

His hands dropped to his side.

"I don't understand you," he muttered, more to himself, as he moved a few feet away from me. "You said you wanted me, and even that you cared for me, but whenever I try to touch you, you shy away," he paused, "Am I that repugnant?"

"Of course not!" I spun around, disregarding the fact that he was nude, and grabbed his hand. Bringing my hand up to his face, I cupped his cheek in my palm. "You are the most beautiful being I have ever seen, human or Fae."

Daring to close the distance between us further, I let my eyes fill with everything he made me feel, the desire, the laughter, even the emotions that I had not dared to name even to myself.

"I think about you all the time. When you aren't here, I wonder what you are doing, and when you are, my eyes can't stop themselves from searching you out. I could never ever find you anything but spectacular."

Raw emotions filled his face, and before I could decipher what they were, his lips sought mine out. Our mouths clashed together, and I let him draw my tongue into his mouth, the distinct taste of him filling my senses. I couldn't think of any better pastime than to be right here, kissing him. When his hands found their way to the tie of my robe, I arched into him.

With my permission given, the robe was pulled open, and he hunted out the skin beneath. The moment his fingers touched my hips, I was on fire. His claws slid along my skin, stroking in time with our mouths, and just when I felt like I couldn't get enough of him, he pushed my robe from my shoulders and brought our bodies flush together.

I pulled back from the kiss to glance up at him. His eyes were full of heat and desire. I wrapped my arms around his neck and offered my mouth to him again. This time, when he kissed me, his tail decided to join in. It wrapped itself around my waist, rubbing along the edges of my hipbones, causing a delightful tingle to spread.

Along with the stimulation of his tail, he was pressed long and hard against my stomach. I wriggled in place. A low growl rumbled from his throat, and his hands left my sides to lift me up into his arms. I wrapped my legs around him and whimpered when my center brushed against the ridges of his stomach.

Shots of pleasure ripped through me as he lowered me onto the bed, making sure to rub every inch of him against my heat. Sliding one thigh to the side, he pulled away from our kiss so he could take me in. With his eyes on my skin, I could feel my face fill with heat, and I turned away from the intensity of his gaze.

"Don't look away, love." His voice was rough and sent shivers down my spine, but I glanced back to him beneath lowered lashes, not wanting to see his reaction to my body.

He leaned down to stroke his nose along the curve of my breast before taking my nipple in his mouth and giving it a nip. I cried out and turned my eyes to him with a glare.

"Katherine, you are the loveliest creature I have ever known."

My eyes softened at his words.

"I've wanted you since the moment I set eyes on you." His voice lowered, as did his hand. He stroked down my side, teasing my breast, before cupping me between my legs. "The smell of you has been driving me up the wall. I want to roll around in it." His finger stroked my bud, making me gasp and groan. "Taste it." His mouth licked at my skin. "Until all I know is you."

I whimpered and moaned, a combination from his words and the hand that set a torturous pace. My hips lifted off the bed as I fought to get more friction. I almost cried out in frustration when he eased me back every time I tried to force his hand.

"More," I croaked out, almost to the point of begging.

Watching my face, he replaced his finger with his thumb while he sought out my heat. Being mindful of his claws, he slid one finger into me. My insides clenched deliciously around the intrusion.

"Oh, pet," he purred in my ear, increasing the speed of his fingers. "You're on fire. I can't wait to be inside of you, but first I need you to come for me, love."

As if on his command, my body seized up, and my hands clutched the sheet beneath me. Before I could catch my breath, Chess moved over me, and with one fell swoop, slid into me. It hadn't been a long time for me, but long enough that his girth gave me an exquisite feeling of fullness.

We both moaned as we got used to the feeling. My hands found their way to his biceps, and I tilted my hips up to encourage him to move. With a dark chuckle, he shifted and pulled back until he was almost all the way out, before sliding back in with a deep groan. He found a steady pace that was just this side of not fast enough, keeping me right on the edge.

With a growl of frustration, I wrapped my legs around his waist and used my arms to help push myself against him as I tried to take control of our movements. When he caught on to what I was doing, he stopped completely, and my growl turned into a roar. He trapped my hands with his and pressed them above my head.

"So impatient. So needy," he whispered as he adjusted his stance and grabbed a hold of one of my thighs with his free hand.

This time, when he pressed back into me, it was hard and punishing. I cried out with each forceful thrust.

He had me on the edge again within moments, this time, more intense than the last. And with each stroke, I felt my magic respond to the feeling as it made its way to the surface. My eyes locked with his, and I watched in awe as my skin began to glow softly. I glanced down to where our bodies touched, and his skin resonated with mine.

The magic made the pressure so much more exquisite than anything else I had ever experienced. Even more so than what I had with Dorian. When I finally shattered, my nails dug into his flesh, hard enough that there would probably be marks on his skin. He didn't seem to mind as he groaned out his own release and then collapsed next to me on the bed.

As the sweat cooled on our skin, the blinding glow dulled. I fought to catch my breath and turned to ask him if it was always like that for him, but couldn't find the energy. He wrapped his arms around me, pulling me to his chest, and I snuggled in tight as sleep overcame me.

CHAPTER 22

GUILT WILL EAT YOU ALICE

WHEN MY EYES fluttered open, I was happy to find myself still cuddled against the feline who had rocked my world the night before. My gaze searched out his face, and a small smile curled up to find his crystal orbs looking down on me. I ducked my head and blushed as his eyes roamed down my exposed body in the morning light.

Morning? I jerked out of his arms and glanced at the clock to see it was after ten. Brandi was going to be pissed. Jumping off the mattress, I searched for some clean clothes.

"What's your hurry, love?" Chess purred from the bed, propping up on his elbows to give me a full view of his body and showing me he was more than happy with our arrangement.

"I'm late for work." Turning my face away from the sight of him before I got distracted, I set to work on putting on my clothes.

"But I thought we could have a repeat of last night." His voice deepened, reminding me of what had occurred. The prospect was tempting, but getting fired wasn't worth it. Probably.

Ignoring the hungry look he was sending my way, I searched for my cell phone, which was buzzing like crazy. I flipped on the screen to see five missed calls and seventeen text messages.

"Ugh," I groaned, rubbing my hand over my face. My happy feeling sank as I scrolled through the messages from Brandi.

Where are you?

You better not be late again.

Is it that boyfriend of yours? I told you that he was bad news and would hurt your career. This is how you repay me for taking a chance on you even though you don't have the qualifications? Your mother would not approve.

The list went on and on, each one becoming more irate than the last. My eyebrows rose when a few of the messages were actually from Mrs. Jenkins, telling me the boss lady was about to lose her shit if I didn't get my butt in there.

Just as I was about to close my phone, it buzzed again. It was another text from Brandi.

Don't bother coming in. I found someone to replace you.

Was I fired? Did she just fire me over text message? I should be angry or desperate. I should have the urge to call her back right this moment and beg for my job back. But in all honesty, I wasn't. My chest felt like a huge weight had been lifted. One less thing to worry about.

"What is it?" Chess cocked his brow.

"I think I just got fired." I grinned and then found myself laughing.

Fired. Me! Fan-fucking-tastic. I couldn't wait to tell my mother, I could just hear the lecture waiting for me. Maybe I could guilt trip her into paying my bills since she was the one who forced me to take that horrible job in the first place.

The thought of my human mother brought back memories of what had occurred with my Fae mother. Things were going to get more difficult, I was sure, but with no job to worry about, I could focus on defeating the Shadow man and keeping the realms from going to shit.

"And that is a good thing?" Chess crawled out of the bed and sauntered toward me with a playful smirk on his face.

My eyes trailed up his body, the grin on my face spreading wider. God, he was beautiful. I licked my lips as my gaze landed on his face hovering above me.

"Not as good as something else right now." My voice had turned husky.

He wrapped his arms around my waist, pulling me toward him, his tail finding its favorite spot along the inside of my thigh. I slid my hands up his bare chest and tangled my hands in his hair. Grabbing a fist full, I pulled his head down to mine, but paused when his ears twitched.

Were they as soft as they looked? I couldn't help but giggle again when I imagined him thumping his leg like a dog from being scratched behind his ears. Or would he purr?

"I am unclothed and in your arms, what is there to laugh about, pet?" His bemusement showed in his face and voice.

"Your ears."

"Yes, what about them?"

Biting my lip, I reached a hand up, but paused. "Can I?"

His eyes widened a fraction, but he nodded his consent, a sort of anticipatory look filling his face. My hand inched up to his ears, and I slowly slid my fingers over them. His hands tightened on my waist, and he pulled me closer.

"Does that feel good?" I watched his face. His eyes were pinched closed, and a deep reverberation began in the center of his chest. After a moment, he opened his eyes to gaze down at me, the ferocity there created a heat that pooled in the pit of my stomach.

Instead of answering me, his tail moved up from its place and did wicked things that made me ache and moan. His claws moved into my hair, tugging me forward to claim my lips in an aggressive kiss. I continued my assault on his ears, and just as his hand inched up my shirt, a knock came to my bedroom door.

"Lady?" Alice's bell-like voice called out.

I dropped my hands from his ears and shifted to find out what she wanted only to be tugged back by Chess. He pressed my hand to his length with a groan.

"Ignore her."

I was inclined to do just that, but Alice usually didn't leave the TV for just any old reason.

"It might be important." I moved away from the tantalizing hands making their way into my clothing and reached for the door. Giving Chess one more long appreciative look, I slipped out the door and into the hallway.

The smile on my face fell flat when I saw Alice. She had used her powers to transform the yoga pants and t-shirt back into a dark blue tea dress, complete with a little hat and gloves. The change of attire wasn't all that was worrying. The anxious expression and the way she kept looking back toward the living room made me frown harder.

"What is it, Alice?"

"You are usually at that job of yours right now, but you aren't." She wrung her hands together, as if not sure of her own words.

"I know. I woke up late. Not that it matters, anyway. They fired me." I rolled my eyes and held back a snort.

"That's good. A princess shouldn't have to work." The worry on her face thankfully decreased at that notion but was still there.

I crossed my arms over my chest. "Well, in this world, princesses don't get paid. Not that I could tell them I was a princess, anyway."

"I do not know why the Fae don't just come out, anyway. It is ridiculous that they must hide in their world." She seemed less distracted and more focused on me now that the conversation was moving along. I wondered what had spooked her so much.

"Really? Could you imagine what would happen? I'm surprised there hasn't been anything on the news already." I shook my head at the thought of it. A national alert would no doubt throw the entire United States into a panic, causing them to arm up for the end of the world. No doubt shooting at Shadows would cause more trouble than need be. "I don't think the world is ready for the Fae to come out of the closet just yet."

"I could not agree more, but we may not have a choice." I turned from Alice to find what she had been so nervous about. Standing at the end of the hallway was none other than my fiancé.

"Why do you say that?" I walked toward him. My eyes stayed on his form, and I tried not to look back at the bedroom door where Chess lay in wait. The last thing I needed was a confrontation between my old lover and my new one.

"I just came from the Between." He followed me back into the living room, and he continued, "The guards are dead."

"Dead? Not taken?" Alice spoke up, but when Dorian looked at her, she turned away.

"Not this time. Their bodies were left where they were killed. Though, some of the parts were missing."

"Parts?" I gulped, not liking the sound of it.

"Their heads have yet to be found." Dorian shook his head, his black hair falling into his face. "I do not know if this is some sick joke the Shadows are playing, or if it is something else altogether, but I do know that no one is manning the doors right now. So anyone could be getting into your realm."

I twisted my hair in my hands, thinking about what he had said. If their heads were missing, it couldn't have been the Shadows; it wasn't really their style. Unless. It was a message to my mother. I had just trampled all over her and her guards but killing her own people didn't make sense.

It could have been a message to my mother. Which, knowing what I knew now about what lengths she would go to for power, I had no doubt someone would hold that kind of grudge against her. Even the Shadows.

Looking back up to Dorian, I opened my mouth to tell him my thoughts when he took a step closer to me. A weird look settled on his face.

"What is that?" He sniffed the air around me, his nose scrunching up in disgust.

Before I could figure out what the hell he was talking about, the bedroom door opened.

"While I am perfectly happy lying in your bed all day, I could do with some clothes, pet."

I spun around to find Chess with only a sheet wrapped around his waist and a smirk on his face.

My mouth hung open like a fish as I looked back and forth between the two Fae men. I knew nothing good could come from having them both in the same room. I knew from the rage that began to cloud Dorian's face, that there was no talking my way out of it this time.

"You slept with this — this thing?" Dorian pointed his finger at Chess. "After you told me you needed a break to figure things out!"

"I did. I do." I sighed.

"What she means, is she needs a break from you," Alice supplied, and then gave me a small helpful smile.

Returning her smile with a glare, I growled out, "Don't help me."

"Is what the girl says true?" Dorian turned his scorching glare from Chess to me.

I was tired of dancing around the truth with him.

"What Alice said is sort of true, but what I said was true as well. I am trying to figure things out. And while you are complicated, Chess, he's..." I trailed off, gesturing to Chess, who looked like he was about to burst at the seams in glee.

"An easy fuck? Or do you mean convenient?" His lips twisted into a crude snarl.

"Yes. No." Frustrated, I grab my hair wanting to scream.

"Then what is he?" Dorian demanded, moving a step closer into my personal space. Chess moved close as well. Looking into Chess' face, he snarled. "What is he if not meaningless sex to you?"

Before I could even think about it, before I even knew it was there, my mouth had a life of its own, and I blurted out, "I love him, okay!"

Dead silence. I couldn't believe I had just said that, and in front of my ex, for crying out loud. I hadn't even admitted it to myself, and now here I was spouting it out for all to hear like it was no big deal.

"You love me?" Chess' voice was unsure and surprised.

Embarrassed and suddenly a bit shy, I glanced up at him. "Yeah, I do."

A dozen emotions ran across Chess' face. Happiness. Relief. Then suddenly it switched to what could be only described as fear, anger, and finally sadness. I could have sworn he was going to say it back to me, but instead, a flirty smile crept onto his face, and I knew what was going to come out of his mouth was not what I wanted to hear.

"That's so sweet. I'm flattered really." He tucked a strand of my hair behind my ear with a smile.

Anger and overwhelming confusion filled me. I shoved his clawed hand away from me and took a step back. Chess frowned at me and then leaned down to kiss my cheek.

"I'll go put some clothes on while you take care of this." He gestured to the area around Dorian and then proceeded to glide out of the room as if he hadn't just humiliated me.

The moment Chess left, Dorian turned on me. "See? What do you expect from a half-breed?"

"Dorian." Exasperated at the whole situation, I spun on him. "Just shut the fuck up, and get the hell out of my house!"

I stomped away from him, not caring what he did or said anymore. As far as I was concerned, he was my past, and the only thing I cared about was the man that had just lied to me.

I stormed into the bedroom.

"What the hell was that?" I kept my eyes on him and not on his naked behind as he surveyed his shredded clothing.

"What?" He glanced over his shoulder, a clueless expression on his face, before he sighed and dropped his clothes. "I suppose I could always glamour my clothing on until I can get some more. Unless you'd like to stay in bed all week?" He gave me a cheeky grin. "Last night was fun."

"Fun?" I gaped at him. "Was that all it was to you? Fun?"

"Of course. What did you think it was?" He shrugged and glided over to me, caging me in against the door. "Didn't you have fun?"

"I thought it meant something to you. That I meant something to you."

"You do, kitten." He wiped a tear from my face, and I screamed at myself for leaning into it. "You're a really great friend."

He gave me a fanged grin and slid his hands down to my waist. "Now are we going to find me some pants or get you out of—"

The more that he kept talking; the ache in my chest became a fit of rage. My fist flew through the air. I didn't even feel it when it smashed into his face, throwing him across the room and into the farthest wall.

Not waiting to see if he was all right or still conscious, I barreled out of the room and into the living room where Mop and Trip sat with Alice. Three pairs of eyes darted around the room. Mop kept twisting his hat in a nervous gesture, while Trip tugged on his ears. Alice looked like she was about to burst into tears at any moment.

I stood there for several minutes, waiting for one of them to speak up. They all just stared at me, not speaking or explaining why they were all here.

"Well? What happened?" I growled, anger still fluttering in my chest.

They glanced at each other, a look passing across their faces, but none of them spoke.

"Come on guys, you can't have come all the way here and not tell me what you are so frightened of." I crossed my arms over my chest with an irritated humph.

"Lady, should not worry, Lady shouldn't," Trip spoke up, giving me a weak smile.

"Okay, now I am going to worry." I turned my gaze to Mop. "What is this all about?"

"Uh," Mop started, his eyes more strained than when I saw him last. "Maybe ye should be sittin' down for this?"

He tried to pull me down onto the couch, but I wouldn't have it.

"No. Tell me. What happened?" My voice rose in pitch.

Mop scratched the back of his head and looked down at the ground. "Well, ye see the thing is—"

"The prince is gone!" Alice blurted.

Mop glared at her.

"Gone? What do you mean? He was just here." I cocked my head to the side, but a sinking feeling began in my stomach.

"Well, it started the other day," Mop said. "He be roamin' round the outskirts like always, Trip and I be hangin' around on our way back to Hatter's. Ye know, 'cause he still be acting funny, when we see it."

"See what?" I jumped in, getting impatient at his slow delivery.

"His highness, be talkin' to the mirror, his highness was," Trip stuttered, his eyes darting around the room like a skittish animal.

"So?" I didn't understand. There were plenty of mirrors in the Underground. What did it matter?

"It wouldn' normally." Mop looked off to the side, before seeming to gain his backbone back. "Except that mirror be the one in the mushroom city. The one that be goin' to the —"

"Shadow's Between." I filled in for him, that sinking feeling turned into a sledgehammer cracking at my nerves. "What was he doing there?"

Mop and Trip shrugged. "We don' be knowin'. He be more irritable lately, but most of us just be thinkin' he was havin' trouble with gettin' ye back. But we didn' think nothin' of it until on the way here we be seein' him with the mirror again. But this time, he be goin' through the mirror."

Guilt began to eat at me. I'd told him I didn't want to see him anymore. That I needed a break. And then he found out about Chess. But I didn't think that would cause him to do something so reckless as to join the Shadows, but maybe he did. I didn't know this Dorian; he might be that rash, that stupid to be coaxed in by the Shadow

306

man. I knew his pull, and even I had been tempted to say yes.

"Lady?" Alice touched my arm. "What are we going to do?"

I shook myself from my stupor and locked my eyes on her. "What do you think we are going to do? He may not be my betrothed anymore, but we can't very well let the Shadows have him. No matter how much a pain in the ass he is."

"But how?" Alice had dropped her glamour and was back to the yoga pants and t-shirt, and she was using the edge of the t-shirt sleeve as a tissue. So much for being ladylike.

I opened my mouth to tell her I didn't really know when a voice cried out. Then the sound of glass shattering came from the direction of my bedroom, the bedroom where Chess was laid out unconscious. I darted from the living room and threw open the bedroom door.

The carpet of the bedroom was covered in glass from the floor length mirror and the wood that covered my window was smashed to pieces. But that wasn't what caused my heart to thud in my chest as if it were about to burst out at any moment. Things could be replaced. Damage could be undone.

The thing that made me crumble to the floor and all my anger dissipate in a wave of despair was an empty presence of one Cheshire S. Cat. In his place was a trail of blood leading out the window and a note. A note with two words written in sharp, elaborate handwriting.

You're ready.

DORIAN

MY INSIDES WERE frozen. A deep aching void that screamed in my head to be filled. I knew the Shadows had lied, or at least bent the truth. I should have known better, should have been more prepared. Their voice had called my name from the dark in that slightly off-kilter voice. I could not tell if they were serious, or just having a laugh at my expense, but I was more than tempted to take their offer.

I would have liked to have said I had the strength to tell them no right away, but it would be a lie. My heart was too weak from years of servitude, and then when Lynne came back only to be someone else, it was just too much.

A different face on the soul I loved. The soul I still longed for to this day. Katherine.

Or Kat, as she kept reminding me in the sharp, irritated tone she seemed to reserve only for me.

I did not love her. Not the little human playing pretend, but I did love Lynne. And I would see her every once in a while when she looked at me with those blue eyes I dreamed of waking up to. But the human part of her was suffocating her.

I could have loved her if given the chance. But it was hard to get to know someone who did not want to know you. Who, while they said they were sorry, and knew I did nothing wrong, still looked at me with judgment in their eyes.

The woman I loved would never have let a half-breed anywhere near her. Let alone open her legs to him. Open her heart to him.

I was jealous. As much as I denied my love of the human girl, I was still jealous of what the feline had. I missed the touch of her skin and the smell of her hair. She had integrated herself into my very being even without my knowledge.

Seeing them together. Smelling her marked with his scent. It was enough to drive the strongest man to drastic measures.

So, when the Shadows called out to me, while I was away licking my wounds, I did not hesitate more than a moment. Their words held so much promise. So much logic to their plea.

I would not be bound by the same rules anymore. I would be like her and with it, I would be able to take her and the Underground back from the Seelie Queen's clutches.

There may be separate realms, but it was no secret to those who had been in the Underground for the last hundred years who really had the control. My mother was not as strong as she used to be. My father's death and my banishment had destroyed most of the fire in her.

But that would change.

It would all change when we took back this world and all other worlds. I would let the Shadows use me to fulfill their revenge, but I would be the one who ruled in the end. I would have my kingdom and my queen by my side. Whether she liked it or not. And that half-breed would end up exactly where he should have when he was born: on the darkest abyss of the reaper's tomb.

Thank You for Reading!

Want to find out what happens to Kat next?

Find out in Chasing Princes.

Don't stop there! Find out how it all started with these two prequels.

Lynne & Dorian's story: Chasing Hearts
Alice's story: The Crimes of Alice

Come hang out with me in my Reader's Group on Facebook!
Find out all about my works, sneak peeks of works in progress, and exclusive giveaways.

Don't want to interact but want to be on the up and up?
Follow me on Social Media

facebook.com/erinrbedford
@erin_bedford

Want to be the first to know about my new releases?

Erinbedford.com/newsletter

Made in the USA
Monee, IL
05 July 2022

99075159R00174